KT-449-601

Cascades

General Editor: Geoff Fox

Jan Alone

Other titles in the *Cascades* series which you might enjoy are:

Far From Home   Ouida Sebestyen

This novel deals with the relationships and responsibilities Salty
Yeager encounters when he and his Grandmother leave the farm
when his mother dies. Somehow Salty knows he belongs at the
boarding house where his mother worked for fifteen years, and
where he now earns his keep. Questions about his unknown
father begin to surface during his stay.

Where Nobody Sees   James Watson

Excitement for Luke means badger-watching, until he meets
Petra. When she starts to probe the menacing presence in the
woods, Luke finds himself sucked into a whirlpool of intrigue and
violence. This tense, uncompromising thriller deals with issues of
nuclear dumping and official secrecy in contemporary Britain.

Waiting for the Rain   Sheila Gordon

Compellingly told, this story of 2 boys – one white, one black –
growing up in South Africa, vividly evokes the tensions between
black and white imposed by the system of apartheid.

Jan Alone

Robert Leeson

CollinsEducational
An imprint of HarperCollins*Publishers*

All rights reserved. No part of this publication may be
reproduced or transmitted, in any form, or by any means,
without prior permission.

© Robert Leeson, 1990

ISBN 0 00 330245 8

First published by William Collins Sons & Co Ltd, 1990
Published in Cascades in 1991 by Collins Educational
Printed by Martins of Berwick

For Mary and Alice

Summer

1

Jan woke with the sun in her eyes. She grunted, turned and buried her head in the pillow. But it was no use. She was awake, and thinking. What was the sun doing, flashing like a spotlight through the gap in the curtains? Her window faced west. Was it evening? Had she missed out on a day?

She opened an eye. The alarm clock on her chair read half past nine. It couldn't be evening, the light was too sharp. She jerked upright, the nightdress catching damp and twisted round her body. Sitting on the side of the bed, she dragged it awkwardly over her head.

It was morning all right, last day of term and the first of a new life. The sun made yellow patches on the faded wallpaper. But what was it doing there? Right now it should be lighting up the cluttered yard at the back of the house, not waking her up.

Yawning, she rose and shuffled along her bed, squeezing past her small dressing table to the window, to pull at the curtains. Just in time she remembered her undressed body and held the curtain in place, while she peered round the edge.

Then she understood. Across the road they had just finished their loft conversion. The old attic window had been enlarged and tarted up, a huge sheet of glass that caught the morning sun as it crossed the roofs.

"More money than sense," said Dad with envy. What he meant was – more money, full stop. The Whitfields' attic didn't even have a window. It was a dark dump, reached with ladder and torch. The house was narrow and cramped even with just three of them, Dad, Kev and Jan.

Well, she wouldn't think about that. The sun was there, at last, even second hand. For the past fortnight, it had hidden behind grey seamed clouds that covered the sky, matching her dull mood as the term ended. And today, at last, she would have that sort out with Dad, about the future. For six months, since – for six months she had lived just for the moment, but only just. Now it had to be different.

This evening, when Dad got home and Kev was safely in the front room watching telly, the two of them would sit down, over a meal, and talk.

She turned from the window and sat down on the bed:

"Dad," she said quietly, "I want to sort things out, the way we run our lives, what I'm going to do, what to do about Kev, instead of each one of us muddling along on our own – yes, and what we're going to do about . . ."

She stopped. In the little mirror a naked girl, with auburn hair, a long nose and wide eyes stared back at her. Jan's glance slid away as if to avoid the serious, challenging eyes, and turned to the breasts, big like Mum's, and the hips. They seemed broader. Was she putting on weight? She made a face, catching her reflection by surprise.

"You're a big girl now, Jan."

Her clothes lay where she had dropped them last night across the foot of the bed. As she dressed she found a split in the faded jeans. Was that fashionable? Well, it wasn't in a fashionable place. She'd have to mend it. She pulled them off. Hell. She scooped a safety pin from the dressing table top, pressed the cloth together, pinned it and pulled the jeans on again. You couldn't tell, could you, she asked the girl in the mirror, who simply raised shoulders and eyebrows.

The house was still and empty. Dad had taken Kev to school, leaving her to lie in. A goodwill gesture. Since the last bust-up, as well as the kefuffle at school, there hadn't been much to say.

Downstairs the kitchen was in a mess. The morning sun, the real thing, came in through the tiny back window, shining on dirty dishes piled on the draining board. Kev's half-eaten soggy cereal, Dad's half-drunk cup of tea with half a cigarette folded into the saucer, a plate with toast crumbs, were all arranged like a border round the space in the table where Dad had spread his papers for a last look before he stuffed them into his briefcase and urged Kev in front of him out of the house.

With controlled movements, Jan placed the dishes in the sink, filled it with hot water, cleared the table, ran a cloth across it, filled the kettle for a fresh cup of tea, cut bread for toast, slid it under the grill, switched the radio on and sat down. The kitchen was so small she could do all these things without shifting her feet. For an instant she pictured a long kitchen with fitted units on either side, stretching to a sink beneath a broad window looking onto a garden with the moors and hills beyond.

She made a face. She hated housework anyway. The kettle whistled mockingly at her and she cut it short with a slap. She hated housework but she did it, methodically, to a system – Mum's system.

And after breakfast she cleaned the house from top to bottom, first bedrooms, then front room, then kitchen, as if driving the dirt in front of her to the back door. The vacuum cleaner buzzed, letting out a musty smell. Snapping it open she pulled out the bulging worn bag, held together with a clip from one of her exam folders. Snatching open the back door she flung bag and all into the dustbin.

Well, a new day, a new bag. In the cupboard under the stairs there was only one left, the last of the stock Mum bought, before . . . She fitted the bag and pushed on with the work.

Upstairs in their – his bedroom – she bent to retrieve papers from the floor and put them back on Dad's desk, whipped his bedclothes forward and banged up the sash window, then ran the Hoover savagely to and fro. The open window let in fresh air. It was warming up, going to be a scorcher. With a crack the vacuum cleaner struck the wardrobe and the door swung open. A faint, familiar scent emerged. She saw Mum's coats and dresses lined up and on impulse she slid one off its hanger, a green dress. Mum never had many, but she chose well.

Swiftly pulling off jeans and shirt, Jan flung the dress over her own head then stared, startled at the figure in the mirror, green dress, red hair. It almost fitted her, but not quite, a little loose round waist and hips.

"I must have put on weight." The girl in the mirror looked guilty. Jan turned. The room was empty, of course. Quickly she replaced the dress, pulled on her shirt and jeans and drove the Hoover before her through the house.

By eleven, house and kitchen were clean. What next – shopping? Chop for Dad and her, burger for Kev. The list went through her mind. Then she was angry again. Dad – I've been wanting to have a word . . .

But no one was listening.

Suddenly she had left the house, slamming the front door and wandering down the street, quiet in the morning sun, across the parade where the shops were and down a side street towards the river path. Overhead the sky was blue, without a cloud. The still grey-brown water was ruffled only by swallows' wings as they skimmed to and fro.

Her spirits rose magically as the towpath took her away, past the allotments, the spinney with its massed thorn bushes and the garish plasterboard cottages with their tiny gardens. She walked and walked, breathing deeply, her mind idle. Ahead of her rose the distant moors, brown and purple and above them the bald rock crown of Borley Top where Gran and Grandad lived – and where they used to go walking, when . . . She loved it. Mum and Jan would go ahead arm in arm while Kev and Dad dawdled, playing guessing games or wrestling on the grass . . .

Abruptly she turned in her tracks. The sun was right overhead. She was two miles out of town. Kev was due out from school early today and she had decided to meet him, to make sure he didn't sneak in next door with those little crooks. Yes, and she still had to do the bloody shopping, didn't she?

Her feet pounded on the pavement of their street. Breathlessly she slowed down, almost on tiptoe. The next front door was ajar. Inside she could hear Sandra's machine whirring away. She didn't want a tight little conversation with her.

As she fished in her pocket for the key, her foot struck something. A battered carrier bag sat on the pavement by the doorstep. She smiled ruefully. Old Mrs Elsom had left her something from the allotment – potatoes and carrots. They tasted great. Jan felt guilty. She hadn't talked to the old woman for what seemed ages, and hadn't seen the old man at all. She'd been too wrapped up in herself, walking down her own tunnel of dull misery.

Inside, she remembered with alarm that she had left the bedroom window open. She couldn't think of everything, could she? Now, shopping bag, purse. Bang went the front door and she was clumping along the pavement again. She stopped at the off-licence and hired a video, for Kev. The Indian manager smiled: "That'll keep him quiet for three hours," he said. He'd read her thoughts.

In the butcher's she watched Harry's huge fingers and knife poise delicately over the pork, the blade shifting a fraction this way and that way while his eyes crossed with hers – not too thick, not too dear, please. Harry knew. Jan liked him. Could you like a feller as old as your grandad, with a broad meaty face? Yes, you could, though she didn't know why. She paid, her mind doing quick sums with the rest of the money, and left. It was gone two o'clock.

There was just time to dump the shopping, and hike down Gorse Lane past Cartwright's where Mum used to work, and along to the junior school. The place was alive with yelling kids and chattering mums. Jan nodded to one or two people, but kept her eyes open for Kev. Here he came, sharp eyes dark in his pale face, sweat-plastered hair on his forehead, shirt hanging over his belt.

He made no objections to coming with her, for a wonder. He'd remembered her promise, approved her choice of video, and chattered breathlessly about some mishap at school. Jan barely listened, but nodded and nodded as the stream of words flowed. A shadow loomed, the dark wall of the old people's home leaned out over the pavement, bulging and cracked.

"Quick, quick," she found Kev's sticky hand in hers. He'd remembered the game Mum used to play with them. Hurry hurry, before the wall comes crashing down, hurry on, and quick into the turning for our street, and be safe.

The afternoon went quickly. She read a Douglas Adams book while Kev played in his room. For a miracle, he accepted he wasn't getting the video until the evening.

Later she cleaned the potatoes and carrots, put the chops with onions in the oven. Five o'clock. She gave Kev his tea and let him carry off the video into the front room.

The kitchen grew stuffy with heat. She opened the back door. The smell of cooking meat began to drift up. She switched the oven off. Nearly six. Now, a new cloth on the kitchen table, and the flowers she'd bought.

The vegetables bubbled, lifting the pan lid. She turned down the heat. Everything ready now. The clock in the front room chiming six mingled with the hiss of ray guns and monster howls from outer space.

Jan drew a deep breath, sat down in a chair by the table and waited for Dad. And waited.

2

At half past six, Jan heard a car outside, beyond the noise of the video in the front room. Excitement winning over annoyance she swiftly served the meal, splashing vegetable water on the cooker and swearing. The noise died away as the motorist drove off. Biting her lips she pushed the loaded plates back into the oven, wiped the spilt liquid from the cooker top and sat down.

At seven she got out her own plate and began to eat. But her throat squeezed in with irritation and she put the plate back. At half past seven she rose and was on her way into the front room to join Kev who would no doubt tell her all the plot so far, when she heard Dad's key in the lock. Unwilling to be found in the passage she moved backwards into the kitchen catching her heel on the chair as she sat down. The smart of pain mingled with resentment in head and eyes. But she mustn't have a row. This was to be a sort out not a bust-up.

The kitchen door banged back. Dad stood in the doorway, eyes lit, arms loaded. He bent his head, avoiding her glance and talked rapidly.

"I honestly had no idea it was so late, Jan."

He raised his head and faced her, "I'm sorry, love."

She faced him. "The chops'll be dried out, Dad."

Now she was apologising. He picked up the uncertain tone in her voice.

"Oh, never mind the chops. We can have them tomorrow. Look, I got these from the takeaway, and this," he bumped a half bottle of wine down, a little too near the edge of the table. Jan shifted it further in. Their eyes met again and his moved away.

"I'll be with you in a minute." He was edging out of the room, taking off his coat. Jan began to open the packets, spare ribs, sweet and sour. The smells suddenly revived her appetite. She put out plates, poured wine, began slowly to get her thoughts together once more:

Dad, there's a number of things . . .

But he was back again, sitting down, lifting his glass and talking quickly:

"The reason I was – a bit late" (a bit?) "was we had this seminar – people on the course, junior management from local firms. I met some very nice folk. But . . ."

He paused.

"There were also some executives from Bomex, you know the big outfit based in Manchester, high tech people, Japanese money, Arab money, you name it. They're moving in here, buying firms up. Some firms are going to be closed down. You know, Jan, I got out of production work just in time. But that's the way with these big firms these days, they need fewer Indians and more chiefs. They're going to be recruiting junior management. They've had their eyes on our course."

Jan broke in, sharply. "Did they offer you a job, Dad?"

"Oh, nothing like that. They don't operate that way. They just size people up. But maybe, in the spring, when I do my final exams there'll be something waiting. What it does mean is I can't afford to miss a trick from now on. It's going to be nose to the grindstone all the way."

He sat and grinned at her like a boy. Then his face changed.

"Jan, I'm talking a stream here. And you wanted to have a word with me, didn't you? Sorry. Right. Now, I'll shut up and you carry on."

Jan breathed deeply. She could no longer remember properly what she wanted to say. She listened as the lips slowly shaped the word.

"I just wanted to talk about, well, for a start, my studies.

16

I'll get my results in a fortnight. I mean – do I stay on at school? Then, there's the money. I need some more clothes and there's barely enough for the housekeeping, is there? And the house. It all seems to be coming on me. We were supposed to be like – splitting that, and looking after Kev."

She could see his mind at work as she talked, holding himself back from speaking, weighing up her words.

"Finished?" he asked briskly and took a deep pull at his wine glass. Jan hastily covered the top of her glass, as he reached for the bottle. Already her head felt light.

"That's quite a list," he said. "Let's take it in order, calmly."

Wasn't she calm?

"First, Jan, the money. There isn't any more. Not till I finish and get a post. There isn't enough, either, for a holiday this year, unless," he paused, "you get a job, like, at Cartwright's."

"There's no holiday work, Dad," she broke in, "just some jobs for those who want to stay on. There's a big queue of girls from Gorse Lane down at the works. There's plenty need it more than I do."

His eyebrows rose slightly.

"Not in production, Jan. I thought that they practically offered you that job in Personnel the other week. It'd be right up your street."

"You mean, Mum's old job?"

There was a small silence. He tipped the rest of the wine into his glass and was about to drink it down when he stopped himself.

"It's a job, Jan. Look, if you want to study, just take it for six months, or until I know where I am. Then leave – no need to tell them you're not staying."

"I couldn't do that."

His mouth tightened.

"Suit yourself. If you're going to have more money, you

need to get work. If you want to study, we're all going to have to do without till I get through."

His voice softened.

"I've told you before, Jan. I don't mind if you want to pack in school now, or if you want to study. It's up to you. You're old enough to decide for yourself – but you have to."

"Mum wanted me to stay on at school, at all costs."

"I know she did."

There was silence between them again, with just the sound of Dad's finger tapping on the table. He switched the subject.

"About looking after Kev. If you want to stay at school, it stands to reason you'll have to be responsible, first and foremost."

"Why, we'll both be studying, won't we?"

He answered more slowly.

"It's a question of priorities. If you're going to get anywhere, just studying, you'll be at it another three or four years. I've got just under a year. But the last stretch is going to be tough. I shall have to concentrate on getting there. I can't have problems in my hair, like that."

The front room door opened. Suddenly Kev was there in the kitchen doorway, wide-eyed.

"What are you shouting for?"

They turned and looked at him.

"Go and watch your film."

"It's finished."

Jan looked at the cooker clock. Gone eight. She looked at Dad.

"Kev," he said, "just watch something else for half an hour. Go on."

"And don't earwig at the front room door, either," added Jan.

Dad glanced quickly at her. She stared back. Who was in charge? He seemed to recall his earlier words. He

18

nodded at Kev, and when the front room door closed again and the television was on, he said awkwardly: "We'll just have to be flexible, won't we?"

Flexible?

"Dad, suppose I get a job. It won't be easy for me to look after Kev, will it?"

He shrugged, "We can always involve Sandra next door."

"No thanks."

He winced at her abrupt response. Then suddenly he got up and began to clear plates, glasses, packets from the table. When it was clear, he sat down again, speaking calmly, persuasively.

"Jan, I've listened to you, carefully. But it's not you talking, is it? It's your mum at the back of it all, isn't it?"

He raised a hand as if to quell a protest, and went on.

"First you won't take the job at Cartwright's. Why? Because it's your mum's job. That's true, isn't it? Then you reckon she wanted you to go on studying, so you've got to do that. Then you won't let Kev go in next door with Sandra's kids. Why? Because your mum couldn't stand her. You're trying to do things as though she was still here, when she's not."

She wanted to answer, but the force of his words stopped her.

"Listen, Jan. Accept it. She is not coming back. She's gone for good. We have got to put her out of our lives, completely, just as she's done with us."

"How do you know?" Jan burst out.

"How do I bloody know? She went off at the most difficult time for me on my course – yes, and for you. If she cared about your studies why did she vanish when you were taking your exams? What did she care about Kev – whether he goes in Sandra's or where he goes?"

His voice lowered again.

"Of course, it's hard for you. But you're only making it

worse. Be yourself, Jan. Live your own life. Make your choice – is it study, or is it work? About Kev and the housework, we'll sort something out. Cooking, I'm no good at. I'm not all that gone on food right now, any road. If you study, it's one way. If you work, it's another ball game. But whatever you pick, accept what it means. But let's work things out between *us*, not with your mum always in the background. That is the only way we can manage. Jan, we have got to start a new life. I've begun already. You have to do the same."

She rose and turned to the sink. He got up, too.

"I'm going to see Kev off to bed. But first, let's make a change here, for a start."

He took the fourth chair that sat under the kitchen table, and lifted it out into the passage.

"That can go upstairs."

Then he moved the table against the wall and rearranged the three remaining chairs under it. He looked at her.

"Now, there's more room for each one of us."

3

Jan's new life began again with the sun, next morning. She dressed and opened the curtains, shielding her eyes against the dazzling, reflected beam. The sky was light blue, with a scattering of tiny white clouds. She knew it would be another scorcher.

Today was the first in the new routine. Breakfast, then Kev to the playgroup. Was that for his benefit, or for hers? Kev wasn't keen. He never was. The playgroup at Gorse Lane had been chopped so they had a traipse to the rec. And Kev did not like walking. Tough. She did. They could take a bus, but that meant waiting and paying.

"It'll do you good," she said breezily as they set out. His reply was short and so shocking she clapped a hand over his mouth and looked round. The street was empty.

Kev scuffed his feet on the pavement. "Stop it," she almost said. She looked down at him and saw that he walked two feet away from her, as if leaving room for a third person. This was how they went, hand in hand with Mum, all that time ago. The space had to be filled. A fresh start. She moved sideways and put an arm over Kev's shoulder. For a moment, he leaned close to her, but then as they came out onto the parade he moved away again. Here and there were mums escorting kids to the rec. Kev had spotted them first.

"I can go the rest of the way on me own," he muttered.

"And the band played believe me if you like," she replied. They turned off the parade and joined the shuffling column heading for the rec. There two young teachers, a man and a woman were busy, gathering the kids into a ragged crowd. Mums were swiftly turning with instructions and warnings before heading off to work. Once Jan had dumped Fatso, the rest of the day was her own.

The young man greeted Jan cheerfully, looking her over with a connoisseur's eye. He was a right one, she guessed, heartthrob of the third year. She eyed him back boldly. Why not? She was a free woman. His eyes were like Pete's. That was funny, for she hadn't thought of Peter Carey since that day weeks ago, in the pub near Cartwright's. He had stood at the bar, joking with his mates, his face half turned.

"He's standing where you can get a good look at him," Tina Ellis had said knowingly. "They're all the same, think they're the answer to a maiden's prayer."

Well, Peter Carey was answering some other maiden's prayer now and Jan was a free woman. She chatted briefly with the playgroup leader, chuckling at his jokes, then took herself off, leaving Kev with enough money to buy himself a lunchtime burger from the refreshment stall.

Her mind turned to Tina as she wandered back through the shopping centre. Had she got that job in production at Cartwright's? Tina needed it, with her mother God knows where and two little sisters and a brother apart from her dad, that family needed a lot of looking after.

I'm doing all right, really, thought Jan. Just another year at the most, eh, fiddle the housekeeping, draw money out of the savings bank in dribs and drabs, muddle through, get by, then we'll be in clover, won't we?

She strolled down Tina's street and knocked on her door. No answer, though someone next door was giving her the once over from behind the curtain. So that was as good as leaving a visiting card.

She wandered off again, out of the narrow streets and into broader leafy roads. Blue sky and a warm sun ahead and the rest of the day's my own. Outside the tennis courts she stopped to watch. It made her feel restless. A year ago before exam pressure had built up, she'd played for the school. That had gone, like the swimming, and the walking in the hills, all gone down that dark tunnel.

"Jan!" Someone called her from across the first court, a lanky fair-haired girl in white skirt and shirt, two rackets under her arm. Oh, oh thought Jan, Helen. Helen was posh and horsey and only went to Gorse Lane because her parents thought she ought to know "other" people. Helen didn't have much time for "other" people though. She and Jan had kept their distance. Jan raised a hand and prepared to move off, but Helen was waving her racket.

"Come on. Want a game?"

Yes, she did, but she didn't have enough in her pocket for the non-members fee, did she? Helen was by the fence now. She seemed very keen for Jan's company. Her voice was awkwardly coaxing.

"Come on in, whatsisname's nowhere around at the moment. You can pay later."

Jan walked round to the court and Helen flung a racket to her, grimacing when Jan dropped it. It was a lovely job, light, strong and very expensive. Down came Helen's first service, the ball rocketing off the ground and shaving past Jan's cheek.

"Sorry."

Helen ignored the apology. She yelled: "Got the District Cup on Saturday and that silly woman Lisa's gone sick on me. Must have a partner. You free the rest of the week?"

The next service spun off the edge of Jan's racket. Jan threw the balls back to Helen. That was what she was here for, keeping Helen in trim. She skied the next service. The fourth hit her on the nose and brought tears to her eyes.

Helen shrieked with laughter: "Wake up, Jan. You used to be really good."

Suddenly angry, Jan belted the next two back. The third time, she drove the ball past Helen and made her run for it. They settled down. The steady thwack of the ball, the running, leaping, the sun, the breeze made Jan feel better. Two hours passed and they walked off the court like old friends. The groundsman was waiting.

"Hang about," ordered Helen and returned with her purse. "A week's ticket for my friend," she said smartly, ignoring Jan's protest. "Jan, dear, I owe you. That was super. Same time tomorrow, eh." That wasn't a question, that was an instruction. Jan nodded at Helen's back as she walked away.

Jan went home. Sandra's door was open, as it usually was when one of her "friends" was calling. But there was no car outside today. From inside she could hear Sandra's machine going.

"That's my best friend," she had told Jan. "I can knock up more in a day with that than those silly cows at Cartwright's can pull down in a week."

Jan slipped inside their house, closed the front door quietly and went upstairs. She ran a bath, dropping her clothes here and there and sank into the water. Lady of leisure. She lay there, thinking of nothing, while the water cooled. There was nothing to think of, was there? Nothing matters for now, all thoughts, all discussion, could wait.

The house was hot and stuffy. She walked around opening windows then washed the dishes and made herself a sandwich. The fridge was getting empty. So was her purse. What the hell? Putting on a loose dress, button missing, must fix that sometime, she left the house again and wandered away towards the river. As she passed the allotments, she saw a small stooping figure. Old Mrs Elsom was busy with hoe and fork. She looked up and grinned her toothless grin as Jan approached. "Come to stop me working, love?" She straightened her back and pulled a face, then waved aside Jan's thanks for the vegetables left outside the front door. Jan asked about her husband and the old woman shook her head.

"Eating his heart out in bed, our Joe. Poor old chap.

Can't move his legs. Doesn't speak much either. But he gives me a lovely smile now and then."

Mrs Elsom blinked, turned her head a moment, then went on.

"They keep promising to bring a wheelchair so I can take him out, but promises . . ."

Jan took the fork and began to dig. The soil was like iron. She realised that all through the dull grey days, no rain had fallen. How did the old girl manage to turn it over?

"Oh, leave it, love. It'll do tomorrow. It won't run away. Come on, let's get home and make a cup of tea."

But Jan had to say no. In fact she had to leave the old woman and run. The time was gone for picking Kev up from the playgroup.

As she panted up, the rec was emptying and only a few kids hung around the group leader. He looked surprised at her breathless arrival.

"Oh, young Kev? Went about five minutes ago with two mates. Said it was OK, they live next door."

Gritting her teeth, Jan rushed back home. Next door was shut, but she could hear a television set going. But that was in their house. Inside Kev lounged on the settee watching a cartoon programme. He jumped, then grinned.

"You didn't turn up, so I came on home."

"How did you get in?" she demanded. First things first.

"Not telling," he said impudently.

She moved closer.

"How did . . .?"

"If you want to know I got in through the window at the back. You left it open."

Her hand went to her mouth. His cheeky grin told her. You say nowt to Dad, and neither will I.

4

The good weather held. Life slipped into a regular round and Jan against her will began to like it. About eight o'clock, the sun woke her, by arrangement. Dress lazily, tea and toast (Dad cleared the table, now, before he left), then out with Fatso to the rec.

Kevin had his routine, too. If the street was empty, he would walk close to her and she would put an arm around his shoulder. Once in the parade the game would begin.

"What would you buy if you could buy anything?" he would ask as they passed the shops, one by one. Kev was quite clear. He would fill the house up with high tech, not red and yellow plastic computer games, but the real stuff. And he seemed to know, though how she couldn't work out, that this was rubbish and that was ace. Words like "compatible" and "user friendly" fell from his lips with ease. When he grew up, she knew, he'd drive ahead, like Dad. And she would . . .?

"What would you buy?" Kev tugged at her sleeve.

"Oh, books, records," Kev's nose wrinkled. Boring.

On the rec, a few minutes banter with the group leader with the warm eyes. Bloke's eyes were a dead give away. He was interested. Was she? Then, on to the tennis courts and two hours volley and smash with Helen. Used to each other now, they played well and soon attracted an audience of the idlers who appear like magic when women play tennis.

"Ignore 'em," yelled Helen. She didn't care who heard. Jan did ignore them until one day as she bent to scoop a low shot, she felt the pinned-up part of her jeans give way.

She fled to the side of the pavilion, followed by a giggling Helen.

"Can't imagine why you wear that gear for tennis, Jan?"

Jan could. But that night she rummaged in the drawer of her dressing table and found her whites, blouse and flared skirt. They were tight. She hadn't worn them for over a year and her body had moved on. She looked in the mirror and thought, oh so what? Who's going to look?

But the group leader did on the rec next day. And so did the two young mums who had also lingered for a chat with him. He liked her outfit all right. They didn't. Tough.

On the courts Helen's eyebrows rose. So did the spirits of the audience strung out along the wire. There was a whistle as she flung up her arm to serve. She missed, bit her lip and tried again. In the energy of the game, she forgot the onlookers, but as she walked off the courts with Helen, along the fence, she thought she heard a muttered "Wouldn't mind a slice off that . . ."

That night she got out a needle and thread and mended her jeans. Dad watched her at it as all three of them sat in the front room after supper and said, casually,

"Why don't you ask Sandra? She'd run that up on the machine in two minutes."

Jan didn't reply but the needle slid into her finger and she swore under her breath.

"Did you hear what she said, Dad?"

"You get ready for bed, Kev."

After tennis, there was always a bath. She wished they had a shower unit. Maybe she ought to wish for that when they played the window-shopping game in the mornings. The list of things they needed went endlessly through her mind, her own wishes pushed further back in the queue. When Dad got that job, would they ever catch up?

Then on would go her old dress and she'd stroll off along the towpath. Sometimes, she'd find Mrs Elsom working on the allotment and give her a hand, transplanting leeks, carrying endless buckets of water from the tank, lifting the withered potato haulms and piling them up with prunings from raspberry bushes into a bonfire. Mrs Elsom would look complacently at the heap.

"That'll go up like a rocket when we light it."

"If the weather holds."

"It'll hold."

Then back for a quick cup of tea and a word with old Joe Elsom crouching in his armchair by the fire they kept going even in August.

"Talk to our Joe, love. He can't say owt, but he's answering you in his mind," whispered Mrs Elsom. Jan looked at the old man, once so indomitable walking bow-legged down the road in his old railway uniform, now so frail, his skin transparent, the veins standing out on the bent hands.

"If we only had that wheelchair, Joe, I could wheel you down to the allotments and you could tell me what to do."

The old man's face and shoulders shook with silent laughter and the old eyes watered. Jan's heart turned over.

On Monday Helen greeted her like a long lost sister.

"Oh Jan, I hoped you'd come. Are you booking for the week? I'll . . ."

"No, you won't," retorted Jan. This time she'd pay her own way. She plundered the housekeeping money, then at the weekend, she took out more of her precious savings. How long would it last? She put the thought to the back of her mind along with all the other things she would not think about. Doesn't matter, for now.

As they strolled back to the pavilion, Helen said,

"Going in on Friday?"

"Where?" Jan was baffled.

"You are laid back, aren't you? School. Exam results. Still, you'll do OK, won't you? I've bombed, I know."

Oh, the results. Yes, the results. She'd forgotten them. She made a face.

"No, no. I'm sure I failed."

If she had, that would solve one problem, wouldn't it?

5

The school hall was noisy. But the noise came from one end where a small crowd milled around lists posted on the walls. To one side, Jan saw a small row of tables. Teachers sat there, coffee cups in front of them, chatting quietly and watching the movement to and fro.

Jan saw Helen on the way out as she entered. Helen said nothing but made a face and a nose-diving motion with her hand, then laughed and ran out. Did Helen really not care? Did it matter to her whether she failed or not? Jan's inside suddenly went cold as she approached the backs of the crowd.

Out of the corner of her eye she saw Miss Maudesley at one table. Jan jerked her head away but knew that she had been seen. She had not spoken to Miss Maudesley since that day when she had clouted Sharon, one-time best friend and run out of school.

And, talk of the devil, who was that in front of her now, talking a little too loudly, but Sharon herself?

"I'm not bothered really, you know. I mean, a career's all right, but if you get a nice job and like your work."

Sharon had shifted a little to one side. She knows I'm here, thought Jan, and moved over to try and get a sight of the list . . . Walls, Weatherby, Willis, Wilson. Where was Whitfield?

"Pete's done well, of course." Sharon's voice was a fraction higher. "But he's not going on to college this year. They'll keep his place warm. He'll work for twelve months. You have to have a break from study, don't you and there are other things in life."

Sharon lowered her voice at this point and the slightly suggestive note in her words made the hangers on giggle.

"Ooh, you Sharon."

Ooh, you Sharon, thought Jan. All this is for my benefit, isn't it? You're dating my ex and you want to make me turn green, don't you? She had reached the board now and peered at the names. Weatherby, Wheatcroft. The names ran together and she had to blink hard and concentrate. And there it was Whitfield, Janice.

The shock was almost painful as if her heart was working its way up her chest, into her throat. It wasn't true. An A, two Bs, even that paper she thought she'd messed up completely, she'd got a C. She was through in every subject.

She turned and walked blindly away from the board, banging into a table corner which caught her painfully on the thigh.

"Sorry," she mumbled.

"Jan," she heard Miss Maudesley's quiet voice. A hand was on her arm. "Sit down, here."

She sat and her eyes cleared. She saw Miss Maudesley's face, the slight smile, the hand holding up a Thermos flask.

"Cup of coffee?"

She nodded, speechless for a moment. Then the noise by the results board seemed to fade leaving a small area of quiet around them.

"Congratulations, Jan. You did brilliantly. Only two people did better."

"Oh, er thanks." Jan was confused. Then her mind cleared.

"Oh, Miss. I wanted to say. I'm sorry about, you know. I'm really sorry." Jan felt her face burn. Miss Maudesley smiled. The lines around her mouth turned upwards. She looked younger.

"Don't worry, Jan. I understand. You had a tough time

last term. I'm amazed you survived it. And I don't think Sharon has come to much harm."

Oh no, not her.

There was a little silence. Miss Maudesley hesitated, then, – "How are things at home, Jan?"

Jan's throat tightened. Then she made her face smile.

"Oh, all right, thanks. I mean, we're sorting things out, making a fresh start. I mean, the past's the past, isn't it?"

"You're very brave, Jan."

Brave? What me? Nothing to it. Miss Maudesley was still talking.

"Will you come back, Jan?"

Come back? Oh, that.

"We hope you will, Jan. We know things are difficult. But you can go far. You can do anything you want, if you'll only carry on, and get the qualifications."

"It's a long time," she heard herself say, "three, four years, just on a grant and that . . ."

"I know. But it'll pass quickly, Jan, if you study hard. And you won't regret it. At the end of the day you'll have a real choice."

The teacher's words piled up against Jan's silence.

"I know earning a bit is tempting, if you can get a job, that is, but those years won't be wasted. At the end you can spread your wings."

Oh yes, Janice Whitfield, high flier. Why didn't she believe it? Why was she silent? Why couldn't she say yes, yes, I'll be back?

She got up from the table.

"Thanks, I'll have to think about it, have a word with Dad."

The lines of Miss Maudesley's face turned down again and she looked older.

"That's right, Janice." She used Jan's full name. "You think it over. It's your life."

6

Next day at the courts Helen said suddenly to Jan, "Last time."

"Eh?"

"Won't be coming down again. We're away for three weeks, then," a pause, "we're moving to California."

"Lucky you."

"Lucky Father. This is the big one. They want him out there to start up this new plant. We're part of the package. He's promised me I can have professional coaching."

"Great. You'll like that, won't you?"

Helen's lips pursed.

"I know it sounds bad. I like tennis. I love it. But do I want to do nothing else?" She shrugged. "Still, I suppose, till something else turns up."

"Hey, you might marry one of those tennis stars."

"Them? Grunters every last one of 'em, Jan."

Helen bent to pick up her racket from the bench.

"Oh, I expect it'll be fun. Mustn't be niggly."

She turned, her face faintly pink. "I shall miss you, Jan."

Me?

On Sunday, Dad drove them over to Warby to see Gran and Grandad. The sun was almost unbearable but the air over the moors was hazy and as the day went on, grew close and heavy. The little kitchen in the council house was hot, even with the windows open. The oven was going full blast as Gran worked on her roast and Yorkshire. Jan would have liked a salad, but she could hear Grandad's voice, "Rabbit food. Get off with your bother."

But there was more than heat in the atmosphere. Gran

and Grandad spoke little and Jan had a feeling they had been rowing over something. The meal went by in silence – that was the Warby rule, eating was more important than talking. But even the silence had an edge on it. At last the sweet was eaten and Kevin, at a nod from his gran, slipped from his chair and ran outside.

"Well," said Grandad, "what's the news?"

Jan saw he was looking at her.

"Come on, Jan, your results, your exams."

He smiled broadly as Jan listed her grades, then looked round.

"What'd I tell you? Our Jan's a scholar. You can go to university with those, can't you, love?"

Jan shook her head.

"No, Grandad. I've to get my A levels first."

"Eh, what a business. Everlasting isn't it? Still you stick at it. What'll you do? Go in for teaching, eh?"

Jan shot a glance across the table. Gran was frowning, Dad was looking out of the window.

She hesitated.

"I'm not sure what to do, Grandad. I'm thinking it over."

"She could get a good office job with those results," snapped Gran, "bring a bit of money into the house."

"Any fool can do an office job. No, our Jan's going to be something special."

Dad's voice was a little anxious. Why he was anxious, Jan couldn't think, but he was.

"Jan's to make her own mind up – studies or work."

"But I thought that was already decided, last year," said Grandad.

"Last year's not this year," interrupted Gran with a fierce look at Grandad. "Things have changed but you don't seem to see it."

For a second Jan thought Grandad would answer with equal sharpness but instead he changed the subject.

"How's your boyfriend, Jan? Peter whatsit . . ."

Jan blushed.

"Oh she gave him the push," came a voice from the doorway. Fatso had been earwigging again. How much did he know? she wondered. How much did he understand?

"Off you go, big ears," said Grandad. "Anyway, I expect you're well shot of him, Jan. There's plenty more fish in the sea."

"Some women," said Gran, deliberately, "never get married. What does it matter as long as you've someone to look after?"

If Grandad intended to reply, he changed his mind. He got up.

"Shall you come for a walk, our Jan? Leave our Geoff and his mum to have a chat.'

Jan saw Gran and Dad exchange a glance. Something was in the air but she could not make it out. She decided not to bother.

The two of them walked up the track from the estate, taking the whippets on their long leads. As they reached the slope clear of the houses ("where they can't get the cats," said Grandad) they let the dogs go. Then they walked slowly, Grandad puffing gently, for the air was heavy and hot. Grass on the lower slopes was yellowed with the drought and further up, the bracken had gone brown. Summer was burning itself out.

"There'll be thunder tonight," said Grandad. He stopped and sank down on a stone, rubbing his forehead with a handkerchief. Jan sat down on the dry warm grass at his side. Suddenly he said:

"You stick it out, Jan. You do just what you want. Don't let anybody try and make you do what you don't want. Make your own mind up."

"Yes, Grandad. If only I knew what to do. In one way, I'd like to go to college. But on the other hand, I'm fed up with textbooks and that. And I'm truly fed up to the back teeth with having so little money, pinch and scrape, make do, do without. I'm sick of it."

"You know we'll help, Jan, love."

"I know that, Grandad. But I've got to sort things out for myself. At school, a teacher told me 'It's your life' and it is. I know I've got to make my own mind up. It's just, I wish . . ." she almost said it, then stopped. But the old man had caught the unspoken words.

"I know, Jan, but I'm afraid you have to face it, she's not coming back."

The words, from Grandad, seemed more final than when Dad had spoken them that night in the kitchen.

"I know, Grandad. I'm on my own now."

7

The night was hot and Jan was restless. Thunder grumbled in the distance and now and then lightning flashed through the curtains. Time and again she woke and lay staring at the ceiling while her mind turned this way and that.

Get a job, stay at school? Grandad said study, Gran said work. But she was thinking about Dad, wasn't she? Jan needn't marry, she could look after "our Geoff". And what did Dad want? Make your own choice, he said, but accept the consequences. But what did he want? And when she'd made her choice would he accept the consequences? She wasn't sure. Dad was covering something up. She felt this, but did not know what. It was a question of priorities, he said, what comes first. That meant his work, really. He was the breadwinner, wasn't he? So first things first.

But was it right? She didn't know. She had no answer. She just felt something was wrong. If only she could talk it over with . . . She felt herself laugh in the still, hot night. Stupid, if Mum hadn't gone away there wouldn't be this problem, would there?

"You'll have to face it, Jan. She's not coming back." Grandad's sad words as they sat on the grass beneath Borley Top hurt somehow more than Dad's brusque action that evening in the kitchen, when he'd carried the fourth chair out of the kitchen.

"She's not coming back. You're on your own now."

Thunder died away and at last she slept heavily. The house was empty when she rose. Dad had taken Kev out for the day and Jan was free. At a loose end, she wandered down to the tennis court and sat on the bench by the pavilion, watching others play. One woman caught her eye, a cool, strong player, slim sunburnt legs showing against elegantly cut whites, dark hair, short and curly. She had style and made Jan feel she had been put together badly, all angles and bumps, and her clothes felt even shabbier.

A shadow fell on the bench. Play had stopped and the woman had paused a few feet away from her. Now Jan saw that the woman's hair was flecked with grey. The mouth was wide and generous, the skin above the lip just lightly beaded with sweat, the eyes brown and friendly.

Jan stared, the woman hesitated.

"Hello, Janice."

Jan was embarrassed. Who? She wasn't a teacher was she?

"How were the exam results?"

Confused, Jan got up and stammered out her results. The woman smiled: "Nice work," she said, then, "got a job yet?"

"No, I'm – er." Who was she? "I've not made my mind up what I'll do."

The woman smiled again: "Want a coffee?"

Now confusion took over completely.

"Er, no." Jan forgot the thank you. "I've got to go – like." She found the blend of cool smartness and friendliness too much to cope with.

"Well, good luck, anyway."

Jan tried to shed her discomfort by walking smartly away. Sweat had broken out on her face and she drew a hand across her brow. Who was it? Not being able to work it out made her ill at ease, and angry with herself. If she'd stopped for a coffee she could have found out, couldn't she? Yes, but who was paying? Well, the woman would have paid. And that, Jan knew, at last, was why she had escaped.

"Ja-an!"

38

She was belting down Gorse Lane, opposite Cartwright's, when the voice calling her name cut in on her thoughts. Across the road was Tina Ellis. Before she could move, Tina had run across and joined her, grabbing her arm.

"Guess what?"

"What?"

"Got a job, that's what. Start on Monday. Come on, let's go and have a drink."

Now they were heading for the Red Lion. Tina had her arm in Jan's, steering her along and into the crowded saloon.

"What'll you have? I'm getting them."

"Tonic, please."

"Go on, have something decent."

Jan shook her head, Tina made a face and turned to the bar. They found a small table near the door and squeezed in on the long wall seat. The noise of lunchtime chat made conversation difficult. But Tina shouted in her ear.

"Dead lucky. You know that day we went for the interview, when you were after a holiday job. Remember that young manager, Thompson, the tasty one?"

Oh, yes, Jan remembered David Thompson, Personnel Department. He had been friendly with Mum, the last person to see her on the day she . . . oh forget it.

"He said they'd try and find me a job and they did."

Tina's voice went up the scale, then down.

"It's probably because Dad works there already, in Maintenance."

"So you're in now," Jan raised her glass.

Tina grimaced: "It's going to be murder. Take our Gary to school and the twins to the minder, then down to Cartwright's. Get my lunch, dash back home, pick up the kids and leave them with a neighbour till three o'clock then back to work for two hours. They call it Flexitime."

"Can your dad not help out?"

"Him? Catch him. He'd be seen dead before he'd do anything like that. Still," Tina took a deep breath, "I'll be earning, buy some clothes at least."

She grinned at Jan, then remembered.

"Hey, what are you doing? Got your results?"

Jan nodded.

"Bet you did well. Staying on?"

Jan shrugged: "Can't make up my mind."

Tina jumped up: "Got to rush, Jan. Listen, you know there's a disco Thursday night at the Market Hall? Coming? I haven't been for ages. Not that there's all that much talent, but – oh come on. Look, I'll meet you in the caff outside – eight o'clock."

Why not? She hadn't been out for ages either, had she?

They parted on the pavement and Jan walked through to her own street. She was mad, wasn't she? She hadn't any money for the disco. She was short on housekeeping anyway. Ah, well, raid the bank again.

Reaching home, she slipped into the house and made herself a sandwich. The fridge was almost empty again. She needed to shop. She left again, this time checking doors and windows carefully. How did you really think about everything when you always had a list of stupid, trivial things you had to remember?

Walking along by the river she found Mrs Elsom and to her surprise the old man was there, perched in a wheel-chair. The old woman was talking to her husband. He listened but did not speak, only nodded and smiled.

"We'll have to burn that rubbish up, Joe. This weather's going to break. I can feel it. And it's all as dry as dry. Oh, hello, love," she turned as Jan approached. "We're just finishing, aren't we, Joe?" She straightened her back and moaned softly as she put a hand to her hip. "Don't know how long I can keep this up." She gathered hoe, fork and plastic bags together.

"Shall I carry them?" offered Jan.

"No, love. I'll carry this. You push our Joe a bit. He'll like that."

They walked slowly back, the old lady chatting as they went.

"It's a godsend, that chair. Joe loves to get out. He was so miserable inside."

She lowered her voice as they came into the street.

"Don't know how long I can keep him at home, though. Doctor says he ought really to go into hospital. There's things I can't do for him, really. But I don't want him to go, I don't."

They paused by the Elsoms' door. The old lady nodded towards Sandra's, the front door slightly open as usual, letting out the whirring note of the machine.

"Madam's changed her tune lately, hasn't she?"

Jan stared.

"I mean, she's not entertaining in the afternoons, is she? Mending her ways."

Yes, Jan suddenly realised that for weeks now there had been no cars outside Sandra's house after lunch.

"Wonder what she's up to?" muttered Mrs Elsom. "No good, that's for sure."

Jan shrugged, embarrassed at having her own thoughts voiced. She helped Mrs Elsom urge the wheelchair over the doorstep into the passage inside the house.

"Cup of tea, love?"

Jan remembered: "Got to rush, sorry. Shopping. Almost forgot it."

"Never ending, isn't it? Drop in on your way back, Jan. Joe'll be pleased."

Jan felt the old man's thin, bony fingers take her hand and press it to his cheek for a second. Her eyes stung. She turned and hurried away.

8

The days slipped away, swallowed up in the routine – seeing to Kev, meals, dishes, cleaning, shopping, chatting in the street. Gran was right, no need for studies, no need for boyfriends, you could pass your life in doing bits and pieces, one day after another buried under a steady stream of tasks which seemed to appear again as fast as she got rid of them.

Routine consumed her hazy, lazy days, her strolling, her reading. It seemed silly to her to break away from the house, just to go up to the allotment and work with Mrs Elsom, or to push the smiling, silent old man to and fro in his wheelchair. Why was one job a bore and a nuisance and another a pleasure? Feelings of guilt rose in her if she thought too much about it.

They were close at hand when Dad kept his promise to do his share, leaving books and papers to attack housework in a kind of controlled fury, swearing quietly at Hoover, brushes, bucket, then back to his room to close the door, always a little noisily. Jan found herself going over the house after he had done it, tidying, picking things up and putting them back where they belonged. But where did they belong? Why put them in this place or that? There was a pattern to everything they did, worked out by someone else. Without thinking she was following it. Now and then she would half deliberately leave things where Dad or Kev had dropped them. Then she would hear his irritable shout (to whom?). "Who left that flaming thing there? I nearly tripped over it."

She answered calmly: "I expect it got left out last time the house got done."

There was an instant's silence, then Dad's door closed quietly.

Sometimes guilt rose to the surface. As she heard Dad around the house, she would half rise to say, "Leave it Dad, I'll do it." But she controlled the impulse and sat down again. She would pick up a book, a text from school and study it, emptily, only to find herself, half an hour later, using a sheet from one of her notebooks to work out the housekeeping money or her own spending, wrestling with stupid small sums, trying to keep the two apart. Money, money, money, bloody money. Would it be all right if they had enough? How much was enough? She just knew she hadn't got it and the lack of it would not leave her thoughts. She was fearful and mean, angry and reckless by turns.

On the day of the disco she drew out from her savings, closing her eyes to how much was left. She blew it all on a skirt and blouse with a low-cut neckline, put it on with an air of defiance, then hastily tied a scarf at her throat and marched out, watched by Kev and Dad. She met Tina and her new mates, spending their first money, smoking with abandon, laughing, with a new line in gossip.

They were friendly, but talked to Jan as if she came from another country. It was hard to believe they had sat, some of them, in the same classroom as she. School was dead for them – as if it had never been. Their voices rose. "No, love, I'm in charge. Give over, I'm paying."

And out of the raucous evening, one picture stayed in Jan's mind for days. As she walked away from the brightly lit hall towards midnight, she looked back to see a little group gathered around a white-faced girl sitting half drunk on a roadside bench, while Tina, hand held aloft, snapped her fingers for a cruising taxi.

Kevin woke her next morning, throwing a letter onto her bed. It was long, white and stiff. It looked important and Kev waited for her to open it. But she glowered at him and put it aside, then dragged herself up for breakfast and the walk to the rec. Kev asked no more questions. He had learnt his sister had developed a sharp tongue and did not push her too far.

She left the letter until lunchtime, then made a cup of coffee and a sandwich before opening it at the kitchen table.

Dear Ms Whitfield – (Ms?)

You will recall that when you came to this department last month, we discussed the possibility of your taking a job with us in Personnel. You were then undecided.

We have again considered this matter and bearing in mind your excellent exam results we would like to offer you a position on a three months' trial. You would be working directly with myself and be involved in our newly computerised system of records.

For this we will provide training and would expect you to involve yourself in studies with a bearing on Business Studies. This is a job with prospects of promotion. We think it will suit someone like yourself.

Can you kindly ring me to arrange an interview? I would stress that the position will remain vacant for only a short period.

Yours sincerely
Margaret Hardwick
(Deputy Personnel Manager)

Jan put the letter down and drank her coffee, now cooling. How did they know about her results? Had they been on to the school? Then suddenly she remembered the day at the tennis courts, the woman in her smart gear, the friendly smile, the curious questions she'd been too shy to answer properly. That was why she was so strangely familiar. She had been the lady in Personnel that July day when David

Thompson had told her all about Mum and her last day before she went away.

Jan snatched up the letter and ran out of the kitchen, taking the stairs two and three at a stride. She must do something and she did it without thinking, though knowing what she was doing. She went through her school things methodically, pulling open drawers, picking up sheets of paper, folders, notes and pushing them all into a carrier bag. When she was satisfied that every trace of her school studies was packed away she took up the bag, left the house and went down to the allotment.

As she guessed, the Elsoms were there, the old girl busy with the big pile of rubbish. She stared at Jan as she emptied papers from her bag onto the top of the brown mass of stalks and leaves. Silently she handed Jan the box of matches from her pocket.

"Here, you light it, love."

Jan did. The pile went up like a rocket, yellow flames, sparks, smoke and then haze rising into the heavy, heat-laden air.

That night a thunderstorm burst and the rain battered Jan's bedroom window. But she slept through it and she dreamed. She dreamt she was climbing up a hill. Somewhere up ahead of her was Mum, she knew, though she could see no one. And as she reached the top, there was no sign of her. She was there, though, just out of sight.

But, in the morning, she forgot the dream.

Autumn

9

The heat of summer vanished in violent winds, hanging clouds, bursts of sunshine, then rain again. On Jan's rare walks the paths were strewn with broken twigs and branches torn from trees.

The old routine vanished just as suddenly and another took over, new scenes, new faces, new impressions, glimpsed as she dashed to and fro, filled out later on as a painter works on a picture, recollection bringing sometimes embarrassment, sometimes laughter. But always new things, urging her on.

That first day, she struggled out of the car, rain beating on her face, gusting wind making it impossible to put up her umbrella, and fled half soaked round the huge steel and glass front of Cartwright Electronics, to the four-storey Administration block beyond.

Later she learnt – top floor, managing director, third floor Sales, second floor Progress-Quality, first floor Maintenance. But today she just knew – ground floor Personnel and she dashed in there, pushing through the swing doors and along the corridor. This time she wasn't a visitor, a Gorse Lane Secondary girl looking for a holiday job, she worked here, personal assistant to . . . she belonged here.

She was early. Had it not been sluicing down outside, she'd have walked up cheerfully in her own time. But Dad offered a lift and was keen to unload her and Kev before getting away smartly to his own work. The corridors were empty, the cleaning women had taken their coats and carrier bags and gone, the first staff had not arrived.

She'd sit down in the waiting room outside the main Personnel office. She could see the glass-panelled door ahead of her. But she hesitated. Where was the waiting room? It had gone, gone completely with its steel-backed chairs and old magazines on low tables. Everything had been cleared out.

Instead there were desks with VDUs (thanks to Kev she knew what they were), a long bench below the window with a photocopier, small internal switchboard, and that other must be a fax machine. They all gleamed grey in the dull daylight.

She realised her coat was dripping a small circle of wet on the carpeted floor, and pulled it off. She lifted her feet up and down, they made dark marks on the grey carpet. Should she take her shoes off and wear carpet slippers, she wondered idiotically. Couldn't stand here.

Be bold. She went out into the corridor and faced the glass door. It was through here, that day earlier in the summer she had first seen David Thompson, the young man in the grey suit, the last one to speak to Mum, before she . . .

But David Thompson was now Personnel manager. There had been changes, big changes. And where did Janice Whitfield, daughter of the woman who had walked out of this job, fit in?

She knocked. Silence. She turned the handle and pushed on the door. The office beyond was spacious and empty. To one side was a large desk with small switchboard, and beyond it a further door marked David Thompson Personnel Manager. On the other side by the window was another desk, a little untidy and flanked by pot plants. A small nameplate stood on the desk. It said simply Margaret Hardwick, no title. Where did Janice Whitfield go?

"Can I help you?" The voice was a touch cool. Jan was yet to learn that these words sometimes meant: "What do you think you're doing here?" She turned.

A woman in her thirties stood in the doorway, blonde

deeply tanned, expensively short-skirted. Her perfume reached over to Jan. The smile came and went.

"Oh you must be the school leaver who's working with Margaret."

Was she?

"I'm Janice Whitfield," she said.

"Well you won't be working in here," the woman said a trifle too quickly. "You'll be next door." She moved past Jan and pushed open a side door near Miss Hardwick's desk and again revealed the room with the VDU tables.

"I expect Maintenance will be bringing you a desk in this morning. You can find a chair, I expect." The door was already closing leaving Jan standing foolishly on the grey carpet again, coat over her arm. She looked around and spotted a stand in the far corner. But just as she moved to hang it up a breathless voice said,

"Oh, don't stick it up there. Put it over the radiator to dry. Come on."

The coat was taken from her and spread out before she could think. Standing by the radiator now was a small bird-like girl, her dark hair hanging untidily over her face. The white shirt blouse was unbuttoned, but not for effect. Jan guessed this girl had been too rushed to fasten it up properly this morning. The longish grey skirt drooped a little on one side as if the hem had given way.

The small face suddenly wrinkled, monkey-like.

"You're Jan Whitfield. My sister was in your class. I'm Penny Castle. Haven't they got you a desk? They're hopeless. I thought you were going to be in with Miss Hardwick though. Anyway, you can sit over here by my desk if you like. Have you used one of these at all? They play war with your eyes. That green light. Like Doctor Who. Still, you get used to it."

Penny chattered on, never bothering whether Jan replied, moving about the office, restacking papers, plucking wilted flowers from a vase.

51

"Feel like a cup of tea? Come on. I know it's early but the weather's . . . Shouldn't boil a kettle in here. Too posh now. Should get it from a machine upstairs. But yeeuch. Anyway do it quick and they won't know."

The tea was made and being drunk when a second girl arrived, was introduced – Lorraine Harris. She nodded to Jan and sat down silently at her desk and busied herself with papers there. She was tall and smart, cool and quiet, a total contrast to Penny.

Maybe, thought Jan, little Penny's talked a hole in her head already.

Jan's desk arrived, carried by two young men from Maintenance who stayed for a cup of tea, a chat with Penny and an eyeful of Lorraine, plus a quick, speculative glance at Jan, then left. Jan looked the desk over. Not much to it. She supposed those VDUs held everything the modern office girl needed.

"Those drawers are stupid," said Penny, suddenly standing by her. "Not deep enough to hold a cup or sandwiches or cakes or your bits and pieces. You're not supposed to exist really." Jan saw Lorraine's eyebrows lift. Penny on the soapbox must be a regular performance.

"Good morning, Janice. Nice to see you."

Penny fled back to her desk. Lorraine's head was bent over her papers. Margaret Hardwick, elegant in grey suiting, dark hair streaked with grey neatly clustered round her head, stood smiling in the doorway, briefcase in hand. If she had been in the rain this morning it hadn't touched her.

"But who put you in here?" There was a puzzled note in the voice.

"Oh," Jan was confused, "a lady from . . ." she gestured towards the side door.

"Vikki, er Mrs Cooper," burst in Penny, then put a hand over her mouth.

There was a quick movement, like a shadow of annoyance on Margaret Hardwick's face, then it vanished.

"Well, come through now, and we'll talk about the work." Margaret Hardwick pushed open the side door. In the other room the sun-tanned lady smiled quickly at them.

"I sorted Janice out. Hope you didn't mind, Margaret . . ."

"Thank you."

The morning went. Jan strove to keep in her head all that Magaret Hardwick told her about the work, personnel files newly put onto computer disc – no messing with filing cabinets and bundles of paper like Mum did – about recruitment, hours, rates of pay, welfare, social arrangements.

But it was all driven out by the stream of chatter from Penny as the untidy little girl showed her round the works.

"Look, this is the old bit – the part you can't see from the road. You know old Cartwright started this forty years ago in a room over his garage? Worked all the hours God sends, drove his family up the wall. My dad went to school with them. Then sold out for five million and now he's drinking himself to death in Ibiza."

They stood by a window on the top floor of the Admin block.

"Look. You can see the old bit, all dirty brick and asbestos. Can't think why they didn't knock it down and make a fresh start. But they just stuck bits on. See, there's Main Production, the big concrete and glass thing, then there's Maintenance Department proper – I mean where they do the real work, not like these layabouts in the Maintenance office," Penny stabbed her finger down to indicate a floor below them.

"On the other side, that's the canteen and dining room. That's not bad. Still, they've got to do something to keep people quiet, haven't they? Then there's Admin where we are now."

She ticked off on her fingers.

"Managing director, that's this floor, with his own staff, his own dining room and his own loo, Henry Livermore, six-foot six, not counting the eyebrows. Next there's Sales, Charlie Sims, he's a bottom pincher so look out, Rodney Mulcaster, Accounts, stiff upper lip, Harold Watkins, Progress and Quality, the women hate him, he's always on their backs, and Maintenance, that's Norris Cooper, nothing against him." She nodded. "Yes, that's his wife, secretary to our lovely boy, David Thompson, just become Personnel manager when old Foxleigh retired. And, boy, has he changed things. All this hardware-software lark came in in two months. I went through the computer course so fast my feet didn't touch the ground. You wait."

As they wandered down the stairs to Personnel, Jan asked about Margaret Hardwick.

"You'll find out. All right. Bit toffee-nosed. Mind you, they all are, including gorgeous David Thompson. Wouldn't trust any of 'em further than I could throw 'em."

And they were back at Personnel.

Almost immediately Jan was called in to see David Thompson. She found Vikki Cooper sitting next to him, as if dealing with correspondence. Thompson got to his feet and reached out a hand, shaking Jan's warmly. Out of the corner of her eye she saw the woman's expression change.

"Nice to see you, Janice. We hope you'll like it here." He paused, as if remembering something, then went on. "For the moment, you'll be working mainly with Miss Hardwick and that's the best place to learn. What she doesn't know about the people here isn't worth knowing."

Again Jan saw the slight shift in expression from Vikki Cooper.

"But, any time you want a word with me just . . ."

"That's right, Jan. Just have a word with me and I'll see Mr Thompson can fit you in," put in Vikki Cooper quickly.

Now Thompson's expression changed. But he said nothing, simply stretched his hand out again and enclosed Jan's warmly. "Good luck."

His eyes seemed to indicate he would like to say more, but the thoughts were kept to himself. She turned and left the room.

But the interview had its effect, it seemed. At one o'clock the side door opened and Jan heard Vikki Cooper's voice.

"It's all right, Margaret. I'll take Jan down to lunch and show her how things work."

Watched by Penny and the silent Lorraine, Jan was walked away by Vikki Cooper. To Jan's surprise she was not taken to the main entrance of Administration but through a side passage and into the old and shabbier part of the works, now only used for first aid and rest rooms and odd store places.

At first Jan imagined they were taking this way round to avoid using the outside covered way. But outside she noticed the rain had blown out and the pale blue sky was filled with flying white clouds.

"The advantage of coming this way – it's a bit grotty I know, Jan dear, (where had the dear come from?) – is that you can get into the staff dining room from the side without walking through the main part. I've never liked walking along being sized up by that crowd."

"Oh," said Jan, wondering, "do we rate a staff canteen?"

There was a shrug.

"Well, sort of." Vikki Cooper pushed open a door in front of them and the smell of cooking and subdued noise of conversation hit Jan at the same time.

The "staff" side was in fact one end of the dining hall partitioned off by a light screen and large rubber plants in

55

pots. Between them Jan could see the "works" part. It seemed little different – tables and chairs, the same, no tablecloths though, lots more people, mainly women mainly in green overalls and some men. And of course a queue.

The staff side, served from its own counter by a young girl in white, was quieter. There were empty tables. And there were tablecloths.

Vikki Cooper looked inquiringly at Jan, who shrugged.

"I'm not bothered really. After all," she jerked her head towards the main dining hall, "a couple of months ago I was sitting in the same classroom and eating in the same dining hall at school with some of the girls. I don't particularly rate dining in a separate bit."

Vikki Cooper's mouth pursed.

"Oh don't worry, I went to the same school as a lot of them. With one difference. I worked, they didn't. I got on, they stayed where they are and where they'll be for the rest of their lives. So I rate things like this. I know it and they know it."

So that was it.

Within a week, the impressions of that first day were overlaid by others as she got deeper into the work and began to get to know the women in production. Her work was about them.

When the men had problems they went in to see David Thompson, the women came to Margaret Hardwick, who smiled when Jan asked her about this.

"I don't mind, Jan. I'm happy to deal with anyone. But the men seem to mind, so I let it go."

"What'd they do if you were in charge?"

"I expect they'd grin and bear it." Margaret did little gossiping and turned quickly back to the work. "Jan, can you please go down and ask Sally Beamish to come up and see me." And off Jan would go, across the covered way if the weather were fine, or through the old works if the rain was coming down, to the great steel and glass cavern where rows of women bent and leaned over the ever-moving conveyor belts, sorting, sifting, picking up, putting down, fixing, throwing out.

Jan noticed that when David Thompson interviewed someone, they were called by Tannoy after a phone call to the line manager by Vikki Cooper.

She met Jan in the corridor one day, on one of her trips down to production and said, "You won't catch me doing that, dear. I'm not an errand girl."

Jan shrugged. Was she one? But she noticed that Margaret Hardwick never buzzed when she wanted her. The side door would open and her head would appear round the door.

"Will you come in please, Jan?"

There was something old-fashioned about Margaret Hardwick, despite her fashionable dress. Jan had a feeling she thought it bad mannered to call people up on the Tannoy. Everything about her was restrained and discreet, reserved.

After a month at Cartwright's Jan knew her no better than when she had started. But she began to like her more.

10

When Jan began to work at Cartwright's, life at home became more frantic, quick meals, comings and goings, like an airport lounge. When it rained, they squeezed into Dad's car, stopping once outside the factory, and again outside Kev's school, and away. They met again round the tea table before each departed, Kev to his station by the television, Dad to his room, Jan to hers.

These brief moments were filled with Kev's chatter and questions about Jan's work – computers, word processors, fax machines. He would shriek with delight at some daft story of the computer swallowing someone's personnel details so that for a fortnight they did not exist. Jan's training course and her alert mind made her swiftly at ease with the technology and just as quickly bored with it. But for Kevin it was endless fascination, his mind a catalogue of makes and terms.

Dad would listen to his jargon-filled prattle with obvious pride, though now and then over tea – eyes tired – he would snap at Jan as she talked: "Oh, do we have to have work twenty-four hours a day?" Then there would be a hush before each of them went their separate ways. Jan learned to take these little outbursts as calmly as she could. She now had some insight into the pressures looming over her father. And she noticed that on such evenings, he would come down from his room later to make the two of them a cup of tea and talk to her, calmly, usually about his work and prospects for the future, as if he were saying bear with me. It was, she realised, the nearest she could get to an apology and she made the best of it.

They nearly fell out, though, over Kev-minding arrangements. He now had his own key and was expected to be home from school in good time, while Jan or Dad had to guarantee to be home swiftly to see he was all right – and up to nought. After some argument, they agreed on two days each week, though Dad was adamant that on Fridays he was not rushing home for anyone. So it would have to be Sandra.

"What's the objection?" he asked Jan. "Look, I know you don't like her but that's not enough reason, is it? You don't like those kids of hers, and I'm not gone on them – two little scuffs. But he'll be in here. She'll look in and perhaps give him a bit of tea . . ."

Jan realised that all this had been discussed with Sandra. It was cut and dried. But she dug her heels in, just for the form.

"It's no odds whether I like her or I don't. It's the way she carries on and runs their home I don't care for."

He laughed: "You know, for your age, you're a bit of a prude."

Her head jerked up. She knew what had been in the back of his mind, though it was never expressed. Instead he went on:

"Let me tell you, Sandra Millington's changing her life-style. Ever since she had that turn-up with her last friend, she hasn't had a man in the place. That's three months now."

That was true, Mrs Elsom had remarked on it.

"And she's smartened the place up no end . . ."

He knew that?

". . . decorated the front room."

Oh ah?

". . . she's trying to give up smoking."

All right, so they agreed. Mondays and Wednesdays were Jan, Tuesdays and Thursday were Dad, and Friday nights Sandra would see to Kev. And so it went on.

Handling the family finances was another matter. But again, Dad had worked things out. He must have been thinking it over ever since that letter came from Cartwright's. She was to pay the housekeeping out of her pay, and the rest was hers. And every month, he would pay an equal sum from his money into the bank account, for holidays, Kev's clothes, and to build up for when they might look for a new house – or a new car. "The old one won't last for ever."

She smiled to herself. Dad said nothing but she knew that this was the arrangement he had had with Mum. And Mum had organised it down to the last penny and had fed them and still kept enough by for her own clothes. And then some back to leave all her dresses and coats in the wardrobe, buy herself a new outfit, a suitcase and a ticket at the railway station to the end of the world.

How did she manage? Jan mused as she wandered round the boutiques and department stores. Mum dressed with style. Jan knew where Tina Ellis and her mates bought their clothes. They were cheap, flash smart and they didn't last. They were meant not to. Miss Hardwick, she guessed, shopped in Manchester, maybe had it all made for her. Jan was stuck in between. Not the nerve to wear what Tina wore, not the money to dress like her new boss. Vikki Cooper, so little Penny reckoned, wore all her wages on her back. She could afford to with her husband in charge of Maintenance. Silent, stand-offish Lorraine came from what they called a good family, so she was all right. And that left Muggins in blouse and grey skirt as if she hadn't left school.

She'd cut back on Kev's cornflakes for a few weeks. The thought amused her grimly as she picked up the shopping on her way home. The butcher's was usually still open. Harry kept funny hours to suit the working women. Harry was all right.

She watched him serving two women, just in front of

her. She knew them, mother and daughter, one widowed, one deserted. They were inseparable – lived together, shopped together, even spoke at the same time. They looked more like sisters, dark gipsy-like faces, always wearing the same old coats well-buttoned, the same battered basket, the same worn purses. Harry would look up bird-like, from one to the other, while they quietly fought out what it would be for supper – six ounces of lamb's liver, three quarters of a pound of sausage, or maybe a chop, "but more fat off, please."

She realised with the new understanding she had from work, just why she liked Harry. He always listened to you. Most blokes either talked over you or kept quiet a moment while they worked out what they'd say next. And there were women who talked and listened to you at the same time. Harry would carefully hear out the simplest thing you had to say, even about the weather and then reply thoughtfully, often in a surprising way. A lot went on in that head of his. Somehow she sensed he was a sad man.

"How's the wife, Harry?" the two women asked.

He shook his head. "None too bright. I made her a pudding at lunchtime, but she couldn't take owt. She can't keep it down. That's the trouble."

They nodded and were gone. Harry beamed at Jan. "Now, Janice dear, what can we do for you – keep the boys happy, eh?"

To her surprise there were voices in the kitchen as she opened the street door. It was Sandra's night for seeing to Kev, but . . .

Kev sat at the table, spread with a new cloth. He was finishing off some tinned peaches Jan was keeping for the weekend.

"Oh, hello, Jan love. Thought I'd just give him his tea, save you the trouble. Had a long day? They keep you at it at Cartwright's. Wouldn't work there to save my life. Sit down."

Jan sat down, putting the shopping on the floor.

"'Course, your dad's late home tonight. I'll just get you a cup of tea and then I'll be off myself."

11

Jan settled in at Cartwright's, getting to know the layout of the works, the way things went in the office, even the eccentric, almost human behaviour of the machines. She relaxed more as her confidence grew. And the more she relaxed, the more she became aware of the tensions around her.

When she worked in Margaret Hardwick's room, she saw how little her boss had to say when Vikki Cooper was there. Only when that lady was in David Thompson's inner office and they were alone would Margaret Hardwick talk more easily. She noticed, too, that when David Thompson passed through and stopped to chat with Miss Hardwick, Vikki Cooper would hover on the edges of the conversation, putting in a word here and there. She seemed to know everything that happened in the company. And Jan saw how Margaret Hardwick silently resisted these intrusions, mouth tightening, voice lowering. But Mr Thompson seemed not to notice.

His young good looks, the easy smile, went with complete confidence. If he was aware his secretary was intruding on the discussion it did not seem to bother him. He was at ease with everyone. And he was always friendly to Jan, chatting about work and home, but ever discreet, never referring to Mum and the time she had worked in the office. Jan had got over the shyness she felt in the first days when he spoke to her, and chatted without embarrassment. But she was careful too, and knew what to leave out of the conversation. She was learning all the time.

She was aware, too, that whenever David Thompson spoke to her, she would get more attention from Vikki

Cooper, a moment's chat in the tech room, or a so-casual, "Coming to lunch, Jan dear?"

In the outer office, Jan found herself balanced between Penny's constant chatter and flitting to and fro and Lorraine's silence. The two girls could not have been more different and Lorraine found her colleague irritating. As Penny gossiped happily over the internal phone, twisting one of her loose strands of hair round her fingers, Lorraine's eyebrows would rise in silent comment, her head slightly turned to include Jan in her exasperation. And this would make Jan uneasy, for though she found Penny's flood of chat too much at times, yet she was not going to gang up on her.

Apart from that, her slight irritation with Penny was mixed with a funny, almost sisterly feeling for the untidy, disorganised kid. Kid? She was older than Jan. She just seemed younger. Penny, she guessed, would always be like this, and there was no harm in her.

There was yet more to it. As Jan got used to the office routine she understood something else.

Penny worked. She could not stay still, her mind swung from one thing to another, but she was never idle. Lorraine's quietness at her desk concealed something that Jan grasped as time went on – she was not working. The pile of papers carefully assembled on her desk would be pushed aside and a magazine slid unobtrusively out of her drawer. If anyone came into the office with fresh work, Lorraine would be busy, green lights winking on her machine. Penny would be chatting to a pot plant in the window and looking down fascinated with what was going on in the car park.

Lorraine it seemed always had some task from David Thompson, via Vikki Cooper, with whom she shared discreet moments of gossip. Work which needed to be done late in the afternoon invariably landed on Penny's desk. Distracted but cheerful she would sling up her jacket and sit down to work, while Lorraine quietly packed away her papers, said a quick, "See you", and vanished. Jan would find herself helping Penny at such times, then almost regretting it when Penny's grateful stream of talk overwhelmed her. "Jan," Margaret Hardwick would remark discreetly, "don't involve yourself too much in other people's work. You have your own, and," she added a little mysteriously, "it will get more not less."

Whenever the work made it possible, Jan would leave the tech room and its quiet tug of war and rove about the works. Her errands to bring women up from Production to Personnel took her several times a day into the huge assembly shop. She recalled the giant steel and glass cavern from years ago, when she was small and her mum had worked there. She remembered it as a cheerful noisy place, packed with women, working, joking, singing. But now it seemed quieter, with fewer women on the assembly line, and they busier, less inclined to talk. One section had been partitioned off. It was known only as the Annexe and there, in subdued light, a smaller number of younger women worked on individual machines, following patterns on screens in front of them. Here there was silence and Jan never lingered.

One day as the bell went for first lunch she found herself amid a group of women heading for the dining room. Now the air was full with the clatter of gossip and joking. She felt her arm taken. Tina Ellis, green overalls carelessly unbuttoned, walked alongside her.

"'Lo, Jan. Haven't talked for ages. Come and have lunch with our mob, unless you prefer the staff side," she put on a prissy voice.

"Get off," retorted Jan. On the quiet, though, she was stunned by the innocent words. On impulse she joined Tina and her mates as they queued with their trays by the serving hatch. Behind the row of white-overalled serving ladies stood the canteen manageress directing the operation.

Jan found her a comic figure, with her heavily made up face, affected voice which always seemed about to ride up the scale. She guessed, though, that Miss Baldwin – she owned up to no Christian name – was not to be treated lightly. She controlled the canteen, its staff and clients as though she were running a girls' school. Her small black eyes switching to and fro missed nothing. For a second, they met Jan's, as if singling her out, then moved on as if she had been filed for later attention.

"She's a right madam," muttered Tina. "Makes you feel you're still at school."

They took their trays to a table and chatted for a while. Jan was no longer conscious of the noise around them, although she knew that Tina and she had raised their voices. It *was* like being back at school.

"Do I like it?" said Tina. "Tell you the truth, I like it less than when I started. It's dead boring, but you can't let your mind wander. If you do, you miss half a dozen bits and pieces and you get the inspectors on your back."

"It's quieter than I remember when Mum took me in years ago," said Jan.

"Yeah. Bound to be. For a start that bloody line's going faster than it used to do. And there's fewer folk on it. So you can't have a chat and a giggle like you used. That's right, isn't it, Doris?"

She addressed a middle-aged woman on their right, who paused in her eating, potato on fork, and looked Jan over with a sharp but not unfriendly glance before answering.

"It's true, love. There were six hundred in the department four years ago. Now there's three hundred and fifty and if they have their way," she jerked her head towards the Admin block, "there'll be fewer. But we're turning out more than ever."

Chairs were pulled back across the table as two men

joined them. One, burly, curly haired and handsome in a brutal way, in his early forties, gave Jan a glance that made her uncomfortable. It was intimate and yet hostile. The other man was younger, plumper, quieter. His grey eyes lowered when their glances met. Tina looked up.

"Oh, hello, Dad, hello, Darren."

She turned to Jan. "This is our dad. This is Jan Whitfield. We went to Gorse Lane together," and she paused, her voice changing slightly, "this is Darren Porter."

Ellis looked Jan over once more.

"Oh, and where are you?"

Jan made herself look Tina's father in the eyes and then looked swiftly at Darren Porter.

"She's in Personnel, Dad," said Tina.

"Oh ah, doing a spot of slumming eh?"

"Oh, give over, Dad." Tina's voice was sharp.

"Do you work for Mr Thompson then?" Darren's voice was quiet almost a whisper.

"Our Tommy boy," interrupted Ellis. "Love's young dream. There's half the women in here'd give half a month's pay for half an hour with him."

Jan kept her eyes on Darren Porter and answered as if Ellis had not spoken.

"I work for Miss Hardwick."

"Oh, Hardwick," said Ellis, pronouncing the name suggestively. He nudged Porter. "You know what Hardwick wants, don't you, Darren?"

Doris turned from her empty plate.

"You've got a one track mind, Bill, you know."

Ellis laughed: "Get off. So's everyone. I'm just more honest about it."

Doris picked up her plate: "Honest is not exactly the word I would use." She turned to Jan. "Ignore him. I was saying, love, it's a lot quieter on production these days. But it's worse in the Annexe. They hardly dare speak in there. It's so much quieter it's unnatural. I don't like it, sitting all day with your eyes on a screen. I'm sure the light's bad for your eyes."

"They get more money," said Tina.

"True, but that's not everything. I like to chat a bit while I'm working."

"Not me," put in Ellis. "I like to work a bit while I'm chatting."

Eating in great bites he launched into an anecdote about the Maintenance Department and its foreman. It was funny and he told it well. He followed it with another and soon had the whole table laughing. It was just at this moment that Jan was aware of people from Administration passing through on their way to the staff dining room. She looked up amid the laughter and her eyes met those of Margaret Hardwick. The older woman looked surprised for an instant and then walked on.

12

One gusty autumn evening while it was still light, Dad sprang a surprise.

"Get your coat on," he said after the supper things were cleared. "Come on," he urged as she hesitated, baffled. "Never you mind," he shot at Kevin as the lad opened his mouth to demand, "Where are you going?"

Dad led the way out, swinging open the car door for Jan, and before she had time to settle herself, he was taking the corner at the end of the street. There was an air about him of a boy with a secret.

Ten minutes later, they stopped on the industrial estate, deserted in the grey light, factory walls standing up around empty roads. He drove into a car park, stopped the car and jumped out.

"OK," he said, "let's change over."

So started their driving lessons, sometimes of an evening, sometimes on Sunday afternoons, first in the wide concrete spaces of the factory area then in the quieter streets around the town. She learned quickly. Only a certain nervousness held her back and made her make foolish mistakes now and then. She was quick, too, to spot the source of the nervousness. When they sat side by side in the tiny car, elbows touching, his face at an angle in the mirror, she could see the tension mount in his face, the slightly moving lips as he tried by force of will to make her do the right thing.

She tried to keep her mind clear of the keyed up personality so close to hers, to listen to his instructions without catching his eye in the mirror, to remember what to do without panic, yet feeling his patience was vanishing with every second that passed, every movement she made, Then,

"Oh, for . . ."

He would explode, there would be a fierce exchange of words between them, a pointless dispute about what he had said, or what he had meant. Once he began, "You're just like . . ." Then he snapped his mouth shut and the silence dropped like a screen between them. There would be slow, painful apologies and then he would begin again. If only, she thought, I could just be by myself a bit I would get it right. Then she would breathe deeply, listen carefully, and begin again.

On the next Sunday, they drove over to see Gran and Grandad. The sky was shrouded in great, grey clouds, streaked with blue, like clothing coming apart at the seams. Huge gusts of rain blotted out the windscreen, despite the frantically swinging wipers. But, just as they passed the top of the moors above Warby, and the great bald summit of Borley Top stood up above them, the rain stopped and the sun came out until the car warmed up uncomfortably.

Dad stopped the car halfway down the slope and said,

"OK, Jan, you drive up to the house."

She managed it with just the tiniest scrape of the hub cap on the kerb and looked up in surprise to see Grandad clapping vigorously and Gran with a thin little smile. Dad must have phoned and told them. Another of his little secrets. If only he'd told her.

But it was a happy day. The dispute between the old couple which had soured the last visit had blown over. They listened to her account of her first days at work, punctuated by Kev's explanation of the hardware she was supposed to be mistress of, and Grandad's delighted grunts of, "Our Jan's doing all right. Didn't I say . . .?"

And Gran adding primly: "Yes, it must be nice for our Geoff."

They drove back over the moors in pouring rain, but as

they neared the town, it eased up and Dad handed the wheel over to Jan.

"Hey," gasped Kevin, "are you letting her drive us all the way home?"

"Not likely," retorted Dad, a little too quickly, "only to the ring road."

All went smoothly, but as they drove down the broad country road past the hospital, Jan's eye suddenly caught something. Just as suddenly she swung the car into the side and braked, jerking her passengers forward.

"What are you doing, for . . .?" demanded Dad, but Jan had the driver's window open and was calling across the road.

"Mrs Elsom, Mrs Elsom."

The old lady bundled up in her old brown coat, stained dark with rain and a plastic hood over her white hair, stood in a long queue by the bus stop. As Mrs Elsom hesitated, peering through the drizzle, Jan leapt out and ran across the road to bring her over to the car. As they returned she found that Dad, silent and tight-lipped was already back behind the wheel. She and Mrs Elsom struggled into the back and Kevin, ever opportunist, nipped into the front.

Jan turned to Mrs Elsom, and began.

"I'd no idea, honest."

The old lady shook her head: "They took him in a week ago. It was for the best. I couldn't manage him at home. But I try to get up there every day."

"Every day? But it's miles."

"I know, love. And these buses are never there when you want them."

"Dad," Jan burst out, "could you, like . . .?"

She saw him frown and Mrs Elsom put in quickly:

"Oh no, Jan. I'm sure your father's too busy to start ferrying me to and fro the hospital."

Dad's face eased, he shook his head hastily.

"I might be able to manage it now and then. I'll be glad to. I'll let you know what I can do."

"You're very kind." Mrs Elsom's face was pink with embarrassment. The rest of the journey was in silence. But once in the house, Dad turned to Jan. She could see he was furious, enough to break their unspoken rule of not rowing in front of Kev.

"Next time, just check before you sign me up for something."

For a second, she forgot they were father and daughter and slipped into her office manner.

"It was all in a good cause, Dad."

He was taken aback for a moment, then answered, in kind:

"Yes, and the road to hell's paved with good intentions."

They left it at that.

13

After the clash with her father, Jan realised that she was really angry with herself. She had neglected the old couple next door. While she settled into her new job, she had simply forgotten them. Out of sight, out of mind.

So she began whenever she could to go with the old neighbour in the evening, or at weekends, waiting at windswept bus stops, holding the battered umbrella over the white head in its pathetic plastic hood, or hanging about in bright, disinfectant-smelling waiting rooms.

Once she had gone in with Mrs Elsom and sat opposite her alongside the bed where old Joe lay, wide-eyed and silent, his fingers endlessly stroking his wife's hand while she talked quietly to him, and tears slowly moving down his cheeks. But she found such moments too much for her and was relieved when Mrs Elsom told her, "Hang on. I won't be long."

Then Mrs Elsom would come out from the ward, wordless and dry-eyed and together they would walk, arm in arm to the bus stop, buffeted by the autumn wind, rain in their faces.

Once or twice she volunteered to go down and see to the allotment. She was shocked to find the neat plots covered with a green-yellow carpet of chickweed, with couch grass moving in from the paths in a remorseless tide, covering the ground and wiping out all traces of digging. For an hour she worked at it furiously, dragging up clumps of weed, each with its sodden black rootball of mud, only to find, next time, that the wind-blown seeds had covered the space she had cleared. Mrs Elsom was less upset than she.

"What does it matter, love?" she said calmly over a cup of tea. And Jan guessed then that the old man would not live much longer.

A couple of times Dad remembered and arranged to drive Mrs Elsom to and fro to the hospital, and a couple of times he had dropped them off, leaving Jan to see the old lady back. Each time she was embarrassingly grateful. And Jan was disappointed when Dad would not promise to do more.

"I won't promise what I can't guarantee," he said firmly. And that was fair enough, wasn't it? Why did she think there was something wrong with it?

The fact was that she and Dad were drifting into a kind of guerrilla war over everything. No, that was too strong, it was a game for two players, not outward hostility, just the scoring of points and the keeping of scores. Quiet tussles would begin round the table at weekends, when the routine of eating, the sameness of the meals would bring grumbles from Kev. When she dismissed them, Dad would intervene, cautiously.

"Give over, Kev. Still, he's got a point, I have to admit."

"You know as well as I do, Dad, it's a matter of money. Making it more interesting means spending more."

"Well, we ought to splash out a bit now and then, shouldn't we?"

"Yes," said Kevin, looking cunningly at both of them.

The wind-blown evenings grew cooler and Kev began to nag to have the electric heaters turned on. Dad would shake his head. Then she would intervene.

"Ah, Dad, what difference does it make, a few pence a unit?"

"It's not that. The temperature goes up and down so much and this front room gets so stuffy when it's warmer outside."

"Dad, it's getting colder every day."

"Just for now. But you'll see, there'll be an Indian summer before we know where we are."

She was vaguely aware that Kev, little devil, was playing them off against each other. How often had he done that with Mum and Dad in the past? Come to that, how often had she done it? And whose side was she on now?

One day, after she had cleaned the house, she heard Dad shout:

"Now, where's that book I was reading, the red-covered one?"

"On your bed," she called back.

"I never put it there."

"I know, you left it on the stairs."

"Well, so I did. So why move it?"

"I was cleaning, wasn't I?"

"I would have moved it when it was my turn to clean."

"It was your turn."

There was silence. Next day the house was cleaned again, and something she had left beneath a chair was placed in the middle of her bed.

14

Jan came to Cartwright's one morning to find the factory unusually quiet. But in her office, voices were raised. They stopped as she entered. Little Penny, flushed, hair over one eye, stood by the window, watering jug waving in her hand, spilling drops as she spoke. More surprising, though, thought Jan, was the sight of cool Lorraine, feet astride, head thrust forward, twin spots of red in her pale cheeks.

"Morning all," she said cheerfully as she dumped her bag on her desk. Neither answered. She turned.

"Hey, what's going on in Production?" she asked, thinking to change the subject. But in that she was mistaken.

"What's not going on, you mean," Lorraine was sarcastic. "They've stopped the line, that's what."

"Oh, why's that?"

"Well, you can find out at lunchtime from your friend Bill Ellis, can't you?"

The effrontery of the words, from ladylike Lorraine, took Jan aback. Then she was about to retort in kind, when Penny burst out:

"Oh, don't be daft, Lorraine. He's not the shop steward. It's Darren Porter."

"Oh, yes, well it's always Bill Ellis shooting his mouth off, anyway."

"You might as well get it right before you start," retorted Penny.

Lorraine shrugged deliberately: "So what? Who cares? I'm not in the union anyway, thank God."

"That's your problem."

"Hey, come on, girls." Jan showed her teeth amiably at

both of them. "Take it easy. Anyway, if the women have stopped work, what's it got to do with Bill Ellis? I mean Darren Porter."

"The women haven't got a choice, have they?" snapped Lorraine. "The blokes have stopped the machines – for maintenance."

"What's wrong with that?" asked Jan innocently.

"Ha bloody ha," Lorraine's voice rose, then dropped suddenly as the door to Margaret Hardwick's room opened. She spoke more quietly: "The maintenance men are on strike. They stop the machines, the women can't work."

Margaret Hardwick came quietly into the room.

"Can we close the meeting, girls, or lower your voices? Mr Thompson can hear you two rooms away."

The three went back to their desks and worked in silence. Penny still looked flushed and angry, but Lorraine, Jan noticed, had gone back to her normal pale calm, except for what looked like a tiny smirk on her lips.

At lunchtime she went into the works dining room and found Darren Porter, Bill Ellis and Tina already at table. She sat down opposite Porter and without more ado began to question him about the dispute. He put down his knife and fork and spoke, as always, with husky quietness.

"It's over. The line started again at half past eleven." His voice took on a slightly formal note. "Both sides reached agreement."

"But, what about the women?" she demanded. "You stopped them working."

He reddened slightly at her tone: "Oh, it's all right. Their union has an agreement about temporary stoppages. They get paid, I mean, unless they stop work themselves . . ."

"Pigs might fly as well," put in Ellis, talking over Porter. Jan resisted the impulse to look at him, though she knew the man's eyes were on her. She kept talking to Porter.

"It still doesn't seem right to me – to stop the women when it's not their quarrel."

"Get off," Ellis pushed in again. "They don't come to any harm, do they? And," he leant forward placing his elbow close to Jan's on the table top, "whenever we get a raise, they put a quid or two on the women's rate next month – just in case they get ideas. But, I'll tell you what. It'll be a cold day in hell when the women do ought for themselves."

Jan raised her head and returned his glance. Out of the corner of her eye, she thought she saw an anxious look in Tina's eyes.

"Well, why shouldn't the women be consulted?" she asked.

"Why should we? They've got their own union."

"You mean men in one union, women in the other?"

"Not exactly," said Darren Porter. "Production workers in one, maintenance in another, and staff people in a third."

"Huh," grunted Ellis, "pull the other. There's not half a dozen staff in a union – except people like little Birdie in Personnel."

Birdie? Jan realised this must mean Penny.

"Seems a bit daft to me," she said, "everybody in different unions."

Darren nodded: "We're supposed to have a committee, everybody represented, but it doesn't meet all that often." He turned to Ellis. "There was a vote on amalgamation a few years ago, wasn't there, but nothing came of it."

"Bloody good job," said Ellis, and filled his mouth. "If I thought I'd have the women in our lot, I'd tear my card up."

Darren shot a quick glance at Jan and Tina and went back to his eating.

15

After the row in the office, life went back to normal, or so it seemed. Lorraine talked very little, little Penny talked too much, mainly to Jan. But the atmosphere was uneasy, like a truce. And, when Margaret Hardwick was out, Lorraine spent more time slipping into the inner office to talk in whispers to Vikki Cooper. Something was in the air, Jan sensed, but could not make out what it was.

One day, Margaret Hardwick called Jan in. Vikki Cooper was out and she spoke more easily.

"Next week, Jan, you'll be working for Mr Thompson in the afternoons – though you'll stay with me in the mornings."

Jan automatically looked round.

"Mrs Cooper is away for a week or two. But you will not be doing her work. You'll be acting as assistant to Mr Thompson as you are doing with me." She paused as she saw a puzzled look on Jan's face. "Any letters Mr Thompson wants doing can be looked after by Lorraine or Penny. But it will mean a good deal more work for you. It may mean working over, you realise?"

Jan nodded. She understood that all right. It made her uneasy, but she guessed life would be livelier from now on.

Margaret Hardwick spoke again hesitatingly.

"You'll still be working from the outer office, I'm afraid, Jan. This is an interim arrangement, though . . ." then she changed her mind and left the sentence unfinished. "But you'll get to know a great deal more of the work."

It was true. Margaret Hardwick's desk was a centre of

quietness, of subdued comings and goings, discreet conversation. David Thompson's room was busy and often noisy with shouted phone exchanges, sudden exits and entrances calls of, "get me a rundown on Maintenance absenteeism, will you, Jan?", jokey meetings with other managers, people standing in doorways with plastic coffee cups held in their hands. The phone on Jan's desk, silent in the mornings, would ring and ring in the afternoon. She spent more time in David Thompson's office working from the low table and easy chair that stood in one corner.

And David Thompson laughed at the idea of her walking down to the Production Department to summon people for interview. "Don't waste time on that, Jan, get them to call the bloke up on the Tannoy. That's what it's there for."

David Thompson, she guessed, must be several years younger than Margaret Hardwick, and she reckoned, about ten years older than herself. He was not thirty yet, but he was going places. She watched him with the other department heads and saw that his friendly, even matey way might hide an impatience with some of the older, more settled of them.

Though he was careful with Archie Livermore, the managing director. Livermore would descend on Thompson's office now and then, with other department heads, to talk over personnel policy. He was as Penny had described him, tall, bulky, with a large, red handsome face topped by bushy white eyebrows and slightly rumpled white hair. He dominated whenever he appeared. Jan, tall herself, found she must look up to face him and that made her feel awkward. He was too big. He knew it and it suited him.

She was asked to sit in now and then, sometimes to take notes for David Thompson, more often to make tea. "Can't stand that bloody plastic stuff," Livermore would boom.

It was all a bit intimidating and Jan felt the need to

boost her spirits. At home, she got out the blouse and skirt she had bought for the disco and never worn since. One was too low and the other too short and she thought for a moment of masking the neckline with a scarf, then rejected the idea. She caught the glances of the managers round the low table as she walked in with a pile of papers she had copied. Mulcaster (Accounts) pursed his lips, Charlie Sims (Sales) leered at her and made some hearty remark, Livermore's eyebrows moved slightly but his face did not. David Thompson's eyes widened.

As she left to prepare tea, she heard Sims through the near-closed door.

"Nice girl, David old lad, pity she's no sense of humour."

A pause before David replied carefully: "I think she has but perhaps she keeps it to herself."

Then there was a burst of laughter as Livermore said loudly,

"Shows good taste, Charlie – your bloody awful jokes."

As she re-entered the room, her eyes met those of David Thompson. There was an expression in them which she could not read.

At lunchtime next day she told the girls. Lorraine looked Jan over and remarked: "Hardly surprising, really."

"Oh, I don't see," said Penny. "Why should you have to dress according to what blokes think?"

"Well, that's what women do, anyway," said Lorraine.

"Do what?" said Jan, her voice sharper.

"I mean dressing to catch men's eyes."

"I don't," said Penny

"I believe that," smiled Lorraine.

The side door opened and Margaret Hardwick stood there.

"What d'you reckon, Miss Hardwick?" burst out Penny.

"About what, Penny?"

"I mean, do women dress just to suit blokes?"

Margaret Hardwick seemed to flush slightly.

"Oh, I think people dress to feel good. But you're unwise if you don't know what signals you're sending out."

There was a silence, which she broke quickly:

"Lunch, eh?"

Still chatting, Jan and Penny wandered down to the dining room. As they stood at the counter of the staff side, Jan suddenly became aware of someone looking at her. She raised her eyes and saw, instead of the young serving lady, the canteen manageress, Miss Baldwin, staring at her.

"And what are you doing on this side, Miss?"

The suddenness of the attack took Jan by surprise. She began to reply, but Miss Baldwin, eyes glittering, pressed on.

"You're on the works, aren't you? I've seen you with Tina Ellis and her father. This side is for office staff. You know the rules."

Jan felt her face grow warm. She was about to answer when she heard Miss Hardwick's quiet voice behind her.

"It's quite all right, Miss Baldwin. Jan works with us in Personnel. Janice Whitfield," she added.

"Oh," the manageress seemed disappointed. Then she looked sharply at Jan, then back to Margaret Hardwick.

"Whitfield? Oh yes. I knew her mother."

No one said any more about the matter, but Jan felt a reserve between Margaret Hardwick and herself. The older woman seemed at times to be on the point of saying something to her, but did not find the chance, or the determination. It remained unsaid, whatever it was, and Jan thought no more about it after a while.

She had in any case little enough time for reflection. Now that she shared her day between Margaret Hardwick and David Thompson she had little chance to chat, let alone brood over what people might think of her. After-noons were hectic high speed affairs. She was learning, and quickly. She felt that David Thompson was satisfied with her. He demanded more of her all the time – information and figures for meetings, records for interviews, calling up men from the works, arranging correspondence. Flitting to and fro between inner and outer office, she tried to share the work load evenly between Penny and Lorraine, though Lorraine, she noticed was less reluctant to take her share when this meant going into David Thompson's room.

The afternoon work began to eat into the evening. More than once she found herself working late, sitting at the low table while David Thompson was busy at his desk. Now and then their eyes would meet. He would smile and say in his easy friendly manner, "How's it going, Jan?" or, "Oh leave that for tomorrow."

Occasionally the exchange of glances was silent. There were things Jan would have liked to find out about the time when Mum had worked with him. But she was not going to ask, and he, it seemed, was not going to tell.

Eventually it happened as Jan knew it would, despite her careful balancing act. She was going to be late on one of the nights she was supposed to see to Kevin. After some hesitation she rang Sandra.

"Do you mind?" she began

But Sandra was ready and replied coolly before she could make the request.

"No trouble, dear. Leave it to me. Your father often does."

16

September slipped into October. The blustering, rainy days gave way to quieter, milder ones. In the early morning, mist lay in swathes on the grass while the squirrels foraged among dying leaves. At night a large golden moon hung in a clear sky.

The sun came back to wake Jan up each day. But she noticed as she lay in bed yawning that the rays no longer shone directly in her eyes. On the wall above her pillow, the yellow patch of sunlight had moved along, away from the place where the wallpaper had faded behind a poster she had long since thrown away. The sun was moving south with the year and the patch on her wall was moving north. The thought gave her a wry smile as she heaved out of bed and lunged over to grab her clothes.

Life was more hectic by the day – mornings with Margaret Hardwick, a hasty lunch, then on to work with David Thompson. Then away early, if she was lucky, to snatch some shopping and see to Kevin.

The difference was that now she was at the college one day a week on the Business Studies course. They'd told her that from the start it was part of the job. They hadn't told her, though, how she could fit it all in, plus the course work, had they? Evenings, after supper, became yet more silent. Now there were two piles of paper on the stairs and whoever did the cleaning just vacuumed round them.

At the college she found the girl students reserved or aloof. They seemed to be treating her as if she were on leave from the sixth form. Well, she was, in a way. But it was more than just being a new girl, it was the way she dressed and talked. They were very cool in their suits and blouses with flowing bows. They already had the jargon of the professions and jobs they had in their sights. She had not yet acquired this, and to tell truth, felt a bit indifferent to it. She didn't really want to join the club but she would not have minded a friendly word now and then.

So she got her war gear on and joined the men students at the table in the refectory. They accepted her all right. Her easy manner and sharp wit sparked off roars of laughter. Soon they began to look out for her, wave and call to her as she passed by.

One day, as she sat at a crowded table during break, a group of older men and women from the Executive course passed by on their way from a lecture. She leaned back in her chair, head up, laughing at a joke from a fellow student, when suddenly her eye caught something. She straightened up. In the middle of the passing crowd was Dad. He had half stopped, was looking straight at her. Then quickly he turned away and walked on with his colleagues.

At home he did not refer directly to the encounter. But on Saturday morning he came into the kitchen where she was getting lunch ready. He hesitated a moment, then said, half question, half statement:

"You won't be wearing that – blouse – when we go to Warby next, will you?"

Without waiting for her reply he left the room.

17

A few evenings later, after the supper things had been cleared away, Dad beckoned Jan into his room. Puzzled, she followed. She thought he was smiling to himself, but he kept his face slightly away until they stood in the space between bed, hastily covered over, desk, strewn with papers, and the heavy, dark wardrobe. He faced her, a smile hovering on his lips. It seemed to make him look younger.

"Look, I was serious when I made that remark about – that blouse. But, I know it's not easy, so . . ."

He swung open the wardrobe door. The faint, familiar scent escaped and Jan felt again the pang of recognition of old emotions. Mum's clothes still filled half the space, hanging on the rail. She caught her breath as he ran his hand along the row, pushing on the hangers to reveal the colours, greens, browns, her favourites.

"I want you to choose – anything you want. It's pointless you going short when there are all these dresses and . . ."

"They won't fit me," she began, then stopped, not wanting to admit that she had tried one on. But he did not seem to realise her meaning. He shook his head.

"Ah, you're the right height and – everything. They may be a bit big round the waist. Need a bit of taking in."

How did he know? Then as he went on, she understood.

"You could – ask Sandra. She'll fix them up."

He saw her face.

"Oh give over. Why shouldn't you ask her? We are neighbours after all and she is helping with Kev. I know

86

sh. . .you can't get on with her, but she's red hot on that machine."

She stretched out a hand, then stopped.

"I don't like it," but she knew she didn't mean that. Well, she did and she didn't.

"Oh, come on," he urged, "pick one or two, see how it goes. They're good stuff – make 'em sit up and beg at Cartwright's."

She felt her cheeks redden and hoped he couldn't see in the evening light. She took a deep breath and the scent seemed to have gone, evaporated into the air. Slowly she stepped forward and slid the hangers to and fro. Well, maybe . . . In the end she picked two dresses and a well-cut grey suit and cream blouse.

"It'll be all right. Just show them to Sandra. She'll fix them up in five minutes."

As she went slowly into her own room she realised that it had all been arranged. They must have been talking about her – and Mum?

A quick flush of anger at the thought made her turn in her own doorway, then it died. She advanced into the room, the setting sun, right way round this time of day, was shining in. She stood in front of the dressing table and held the green dress in front of her, then the brown, then the suit jacket. She saw herself from the outside, a new person, someone she hadn't met before, quite different from the Jan who had gone to school in the summer. She lifted her hair at the back of her neck and let it fall again. She'd do it.

Next day she stood in Sandra's front room. Behind them in the kitchen the television blasted away. A head poked round the inner door, eyes staring insolently at her. Sandra snapped.

"Clear off, there's nowt for you here."

The boy's eyes did not move. He looked Jan up and down. The brat was only ten-eleven, she thought, one of those kids who've seen too much and think they know everything.

Sandra moved suddenly, voice rising.

"Will you get?"

The head vanished round the doorway. Sandra slammed the door and turned, adjusting her expression, though not before Jan had caught a glimpse of pure hatred. Then Sandra masked it with a professional smile.

"Now let's see. What, just the two dresses and the suit?" then she checked herself. "Still, you've picked good stuff. Come and stand over here by the mirror." She held the dress against Jan, nodding to herself, then threw it over the end of the sofa.

"Hm hm. No problem." She waved at Jan. "Just take those off."

Jan looked at the kitchen door.

"Oh don't worry about them."

Sandra shrugged and walking across the room heaved a small table in front of the door and jammed it under the handle. All her movements were quick, almost feverish. She turned again.

"That do you?"

Jan took off the blouse and skirt. She felt shy and girlish, though it was a woman's body looking back at her from the tall mirror on the wall. Sandra snatched up the tape measure from beside her machine and ran it round her body, once, twice, three times.

"You're the same as me, almost, except up there. I'm mostly Marks and Sparks, but you're a big girl, like."

Quickly she swung up the green dress and dropped it lightly over Jan's shoulders and pinched it in at the back.

"Now just look at that. Couple of inches, even less and it's a perfect fit. No one'll know you didn't buy it yourself. The cut'll last for years.

"Your . . ." she hesitated, then whipped the dress up again. "Oh, I don't know why I'm talking in code. Try this other one on." She passed Jan the brown dress, then perched on the arm of the settee.

"Val had style, always. Even when she hadn't two pennies to rub together, she always dressed well. She had the figure for it too, and the walk, what's more. Long strides and her bottom used to sway when she walked. Blokes couldn't take their eyes off. You've got the same walk. Did you know?" She laughed harshly. "'Course you do. Girls always do. They pretend they don't know what effect they have on fellers. But that's the name of the game, isn't it?"

Was it? Jan didn't know. She'd never thought about the way she walked. Walking was getting around, not showing your bum off. Now she felt exposed and embarrassed. But Sandra wasn't even looking at her, she was pulling at the seams of the green dress.

"No problem. Get the suit on, Jan, dear. That's it. That'll make 'em sit up and beg at Cartwright's."

Oh, they'd been talking about her all right. Oh, what the hell? Sandra's thoughts were off in another direction.

"We were all about twenty then. There were upwards of a thousand women working in Cartwright's. We had smashing parties, just before New Year and at Midsummer. 'Course we were mostly women, so they used to invite the blokes from Bonner's. Your dad and my Frank came. He wasn't my Frank then of course. Wish he never had been, the sod. Your dad was a great dancer, lovely little mover except he wasn't little, he was tall. Just what the doctor ordered. I wasn't the only one who fancied him, in fact there might have been a few eyes scratched out, you know what women are like.

"Only Val turned up out of nowhere, from further up north somewhere. They reckoned she'd run off from home when she was fifteen and she'd been moving around ever since. She knew what she wanted and when Geoff your dad spotted her, the rest of us were nowhere. Before we knew, they were getting married . . . pretty quickly."

She put a hand up to her mouth.

"Mustn't tell tales out of school, must I?"

She piled up the dresses while Jan got back into her own clothes.

"Ready by Thursday. Drop in and we'll try them on. Oh forget that," she ran on as Jan offered to pay. "We are family friends, aren't we?"

Jan heard her own voice, flat and sharp at the edges: "If you don't mind. I'd be a lot happier if I paid. If I had to buy them new . . ."

"Suit yourself," Sandra paused. "Just like Val, will of your own. See you Thursday."

18

The following week, Margaret Hardwick invited Jan to move into her room and take over Vikki Cooper's desk. She smiled at her surprise.

"You'll find it quite empty. Mrs Cooper has moved her things out. She'll not be coming back. She's taking over as Mr Livermore's PA."

She paused and looked at Jan.

"I like your new dress. It suits you."

There was a moment's pause, as if Margaret Hardwick were thinking, better than that blouse you were wearing the other day. But she smiled and went on, nodding towards the desk.

"I'm glad. This is the best arrangement. Much more appropriate to your work."

Was she thinking about the dress as well? Jan pushed the thought away and went into the outer office and began to move her few belongings from her drawer. Penny greeted her warmly, but said wistfully: "You'll come in and see your old friends now and then, won't you?"

"Don't be so daft," returned Jan. They grinned at one another.

Lorraine stood up, slapped her papers together and marched out of the room. Penny looked at the door as it closed behind her and giggled.

"Oh, don't mind her," she said. "Madam has had a small disappointment."

"What d'you mean?"

Penny looked at both doors. They were closed. But she lowered her voice.

"Lorraine and Vikki Cooper have always been," she

crossed her fingers, "like that. When Vikki Cooper was old Foxleigh's secretary, she already had her eye on the big one – you know PA to the MD, and she'd more or less promised Lorraine that when she moved up the ladder Lorraine would get her job."

"Get away."

"I kid you not. Being married (sort of) to Norris Cooper, you know head of Maintenance, Vikki always reckoned she could fix anything. But David Thompson must have had other ideas." Penny's voice sank even lower and she came closer to Jan: "You know, Jan, when your mother worked here – she was a smashing lady – I think David Thompson wanted her as his PA, but there was no way he could shift Vikki Cooper. She always got her own way, one way or another. But there was no way he was going to have Lorraine wished on him when Madam moved on."

"Oh, why's that?"

"'Cause he's a workaholic, that's what, and he can't abide people when they sit on their bums all day. That's why he liked your mum, you know, she worked, she was so smart."

Penny stopped and looked at Jan in sudden distress.

"Oh, I'm sorry, Jan. You don't want to talk about this, do you?"

No, no, no.

Penny moved close to Jan.

"I'm glad you're here, Jan. It's nice to have someone in the office who doesn't think about Number One all the time. But . . ." her voice became a whisper, "just watch your back while Madam's around." She flicked a quick glance at the third desk as the door opened suddenly and Lorraine returned. Jan turned to clearing her own desk and Penny moved over to the window. Jan caught a quick, malevolent look on Lorraine's face. But it was aimed at

Penny, not Jan. Had she been listening outside the door? Jan shrugged inwardly and moved away to the inner office.

As the days passed the work absorbed her, increasing as it did little by little. She moved around the works. She avoided using the Tannoy to call people up for interview. In that little battle, Margaret Hardwick's style won out over David Thompson's. But she was not conscious of any tug between them. She just expanded her day to keep up with both. She came in earlier in the mornings, cut down on lunch hours, stayed later in the evenings. She lost count of the days as she became more conscious of the hands on the clock.

There was no time to talk at lunch. Her chats with Tina Ellis, her father and Darren Porter stopped completely. It was not, she told herself, that the exchange with Miss Baldwin in the canteen had changed her views. She still thought separate dining rooms ridiculous. It had just become convenient and more natural to walk down with Margaret Hardwick and continue their conversation in the dining room.

Once, on the works, she met Tina and stopped for a brief chat.

"Haven't seen you in the canteen lately," said Tina, running an eye over Jan's dress. "Going up market, are we?"

"Give over," said Jan. "I just haven't time to breathe."

They laughed, but Jan felt uncomfortable afterwards.

Sometimes she would miss out on her lunch hour and eat sandwiches in David Thompson's room while they ran through reports and statistics together. She could see that he approved of her new wardrobe, men's eyes sent very clear signals. But he allowed himself no idle conversation while they worked. But, now and then, as the afternoon drew to a close and Margaret Hardwick called "Good night" from the other room as she left, the two of them would pause for a breather and he would ask:

93

"Like the work, Jan?"

She looked at him. Their eyes crossed. She looked away, then nodded.

"Are you sure we're not working you too hard?"

"Don't mind." If only she could look straight at him and talk easily now that they were alone together.

"You'll just have to let me know if the going gets heavy. It is just that you have picked up the work so quickly, as if you were born to it."

There was a quick laugh from both of them.

"It's a relief to be able to depend on someone else to do things without being told to."

He broke off as if he had nearly said more than he should. They went back to the work, then suddenly he slipped his papers together.

"Oh, I'll take these. I have had enough of Cartwright Electronics for today. Fancy a coffee, Jan? No, I mean a real cup."

The invitation was run into the sentence so smoothly that she had said "Yes" before she knew her mouth had opened. And she was on her feet too, collecting her papers. Outside the corridors were deserted. The car park too was empty. He breathed in.

"Lovely evening."

The sun cast long shadows and shone blindingly into the car as they drove away, heading for the other side of town. The air was fresh, even warm as they walked into a small old-fashioned café of the tea-room type. She had never been in there before. It was expensive and discreet with deep armchairs and the coffee was really good. Now they chatted easily. The time went by quickly.

Only as he dropped her off, a little way from her street, he suddenly said, very quietly:

"Do you ever hear anything of Va . . . of your mother?"

She shook her head.

"Nothing. I don't really think about it, you know."

94

"Sorry. Didn't mean to . . ."

"Doesn't matter. Good night, and thanks for the coffee."

"Good night, Jan."

19

For Jan there were not enough hours in the day now. If she were only two people, she thought, she could handle it all, at work and at home. Sometimes she felt she was two people, each leading separate lives, one bold and capable, moving swiftly down corridors at work, pausing briefly to chat, to pass on a message, to tap data from a machine, the other hurried and harassed, rushing here and there, making tea, supper, doing the shopping, cleaning, making lists and adding up pounds and pence.

And there was also a third Jan, who slipped away at night to dream strange turbulent dreams, or walk by herself along the river or through the park. Sometimes, at weekends, she slipped out early and saw the sun come up golden behind the massive arms of the oak trees, dew on the grass and yellow pools of leaves at the foot of the horse chestnuts. She saw for the first time how some trees took on their autumn colours before others, how on one tree a patch of leaves would turn before the rest, and how the topmost branches began to stand out bare.

This third, private Jan watched things around her, kept an eye on the work Jan and the home Jan, saw things that they ignored or forgot and sometimes thought about things they did not wish to know. This Jan noticed the look in David Thompson's eyes, and the questioning lift of Margaret Hardwick's eyebrow. She caught the bleak look in old Mrs Elsom's face as they passed on the street in the evenings as her neighbour made the weary journey to the hospital. And now and then, this Jan saw Mum in her dreams, standing so close to the bed she could almost be touched.

Once, in the butcher's, she noticed a young woman, just a year or two older than herself, pregnant stomach curving outwards through the folds in her dress, a girl still, but soon a mother. And she wondered, was that how Mum looked when she had me?

She escaped these thoughts by pushing herself into the routine of housework, shopping, even gossiping. She would stop to talk to Harry, asking him about his wife, chatting about the weather, about food, about holidays. But once, as she hurried into the shop on the way home from work, wearing the grey suit Sandra had altered for her, Harry had looked up and, in a moment's confusion said, "Good evening, Mrs W . . ." Then he had turned round and busied himself at the bench behind the counter to hide his mistake.

Twice she made time to go with Mrs Elsom to the hospital. The old lady said little, only clinging a little tighter to Jan's arm as they walked down the street. Jan went two or three times to the allotment, dug vegetables and left them in a carrier on her neighbour's doorstep. She could see that soon the creeping weeds would cover all the carefully tended ground.

But the old woman just shrugged and said: "It'll have to see to itself, Jan love. I do what I can, and what I can't I'll leave."

There was something else, though, that the private Jan watched with growing anxiety and resentment, and that was the way Sandra was moving in on their lives, or letting her life blend and blur with theirs. Some weeks, looking after Kevin had been taken over almost entirely by Sandra. Jan would come home to find her in the front room with Kevin, turning swiftly to stub out a cigarette or offer a cup of tea. Or she would rush home to find the house in darkness and Kev next door in the crowded, smoke-filled kitchen with Sandra's insolent boys. She was vaguely aware that Kev was putting on weight, his face growing puffy as he stuffed himself on cake and chocolate at Sandra's.

More sharply she was conscious that her brother's sharp little mind became more knowing, his liking for adult TV more open. His sniggers and sidelong glances at jokes and references half understood were more open too. His snub nose would wrinkle in contempt at Jan's choice of video from the off-licence. What was the little devil watching next door?

She tried to voice her worries with Dad, though finding time to talk was not easy. They spent less and less time together. Even the driving lessons had begun to take place less often and sometimes these were so fraught with tensions and unspoken dispute that she was half relieved when they did not take place. But late one evening when they sat in the kitchen over a sandwich, both tired and brooding over their studies, she pulled herself together and tackled him about her brother.

Dad shrugged as she hesitatingly set out her concerns, then calmly batted them back like a bored tennis player. "Oh, his weight goes up and down. He'll run it off come summer, you'll see." Then, "What do you want, Jan? You're bothered if he stays next door. And for some reason you get offended if she slips in here and makes his tea. We're lucky to have a good neighbour."

She must have pulled a face. He leaned forward.

"Look, either Cartwright's Personnel can manage with less overtime or you have to put up with the situation. Incidentally," he said, suddenly switching his line of attack, "do you really have to work over so often? I mean, is it so important?"

Important? She felt a surge of anger, then embarrassment. Was it vital to have that evening cup of coffee with David Thompson? No, she wasn't discussing that, even with herself. Calmly she said, "Just now, when I'm getting

98

into the work, Dad, I think it is important. By next year, things should be easier."

He stared at her. Without thinking she had played his own words back to him. Next year, everything would be different, everything would be better – more money, more everything. Next year, there'd be a new life, wouldn't there? So why bother too much about Kev, his behaviour wasn't too outrageous, was it? Why bother about Sandra? It was only for a while.

Dad spoke:

"Yes, I think on the whole, we're managing not too badly and if Sandra likes to help out, why knock it?"

Why? But what's in it for Sandra? The question stayed unasked.

And why was Jan so resentful of Sandra and her intrusion into their life and home? If that question was in Dad's mind, he did not voice it either.

20

It was Sunday morning and they were getting ready for the visit to Warby. It seemed amazing that a month had gone by. Jan stood by her mirror looking at herself in the green dress, fiddling with earrings and trying to make a choice, when Dad tapped on her bedroom door.

"Jan, love, would you mind very much taking Kev to Warby on the bus? I've really got to have a blitz on this work and this is the first clear day I've had."

She sat down on the bed. He did not come in, but pushed the door slightly open and continued to speak from behind it.

"I'll pick you up this afternoon – no problem."

A pause

"It's OK. I've told Gran already."

Oh well, it's all right then. If Gran's happy. She shrugged towards the door.

"I don't mind, but what about Fatso? He is going to be very stroppy."

"I'll have a word with him. Anyway, a bit of a walk to and fro the bus stop will do him good."

He gave a half laugh. "You said he was overweight."

As she reached the door, Dad had retreated into his own room. But Kevin, blear-eyed and furious, in rumpled pyjamas, stood on the landing glaring at her. Was it her fault, already?

It was cold and misty when they set out and Kevin grumbled non-stop. She let him run on – what was the point of arguing? Anyway, she sympathised with him. She took his moaning calmly. It would be great, she thought, as they stood in the empty bus shelter while Kev stamped and kicked a discarded beer can, if one could always take everything calmly, as though it were happening to someone else. She became absorbed in her coat – it was too short for the green dress, a woman growing out of a girl's shell. She must have a new coat. But when? Next year? It would all happen next year.

Kevin, tired of nagging at her, suddenly nudged her. She looked up in surprise as the bus ground in to the kerb and the door slid open. Inside they sat in silence, Kev's nose against the steamed window until the town was behind them and the bus struggling up the moor road. Suddenly Kev spoke

"Something beginning with 'S'."

"Sausage."

He giggled: "Get off."

"Skyscraper."

"Dah. Look – sparrowhawk."

She looked up. The mist had gone, the sky was a clear, clear blue and the sun was blinding down the hill road and filling the bus and its worn plastic seating with orange-yellow light. The moors were golden brown and purple, and there up in front like a giant bald head, was Borley Top.

"Something beginning with 'G'," she said.

"Horse," he answered.

"Oh, very witty."

"Geranium."

"My foot."

"There was, in that cottage garden."

"It's to be something that's in view all the time."

"Oh, you're making up rules. That's not on."

"'Course it is."

"Why?"

"'Cause I'm bigger than you."

He pushed her. They were wrestling when the bus pulled up.

"Warby," called the conductor.

They scrambled out and wandered down the track to the estate. She put an arm round Kev's shoulder, and as always when they were on their own he pulled into her and pressed the side of his face into her coat.

Grandad was waiting at the gate. He bent to kiss Kev, then looked up at her. The coat was open and he could see the green dress. His eyes were puzzled as if he felt he had seen it before but could not remember. Not so with Gran.

She turned from the mantelpiece where she had been bending over the fire, and stared open-mouthed as Jan, coat off, stood in the kitchen doorway. The mouth closed in a tight line as Grandad and Kevin followed Jan in.

"What d'you reckon to Jan's new dress?"

"Very nice."

Gran said no more. She remembered that dress all right. And Jan had an uneasy feeling about what strange thoughts had passed through her head in that split second.

"Sorry Dad can't be here. He was just too busy."

Gran nodded. "I'll put some gooseberry pie in a dish and you can take it back for him."

After the silent Sunday meal, Jan and Grandad chatted about her work. He was keen to hear her stories, but Gran busied herself in clearing the table. She was uneasy with any talk of work which did not concern "our Geoff". But Jan felt there was something a little bit more behind this. There was something between Gran and Grandad and it had to do with her.

It was a relief when Grandad stood up and said:

"Let's walk the whippets up the brew, eh?"

"I'll help Gran with the washing up first."

"There's no need," said Gran from the kitchen, but Jan insisted. She took the tea towel from its rail and began to pick up dishes as Gran piled them up. As she moved to and fro, she could tell she was being watched. And she knew it was the dress. Then the thought flooded through her: when she had come through the kitchen door, did Gran think, just for that instant, that it was Mum standing there in the green dress? But that was impossible. She wasn't so like Mum, was she?

"No need to polish 'em," said Gran tartly. Jan realised she had been twisting the same plate round and round in the cloth. She smiled self-consciously and put the plate down.

When she stood outside putting on her coat she saw Kevin standing by Grandad, holding one of the dogs.

"Wonders'll never cease," she said

"Don't be sarky," muttered her brother.

Grandad grinned apologetically.

"It was my idea. I said he ought to come with us. Bit of a walk will do the lad good."

He poked Kev playfully in the middle and they set off, the lad running ahead of them holding the long leather strap clipped to the dog's collar. When they were clear of the house, Grandad began to question Jan about work again, as they made their way up the track to the moors. He listened keenly, putting in a word now and then, as if he were storing up what she said rather than just chatting.

On the lower slopes the dogs went free. Kev began to drop behind but to Jan's surprise, Grandad turned and called him to come on.

"Oh, it doesn't matter Grandad," she said, "He can wait for us on the way back. He's never liked walking."

"That's his trouble. He's too fat for his own good." He shouted, "Come on, lad. Just a bit further."

Kevin grumbled and reluctantly caught up with them. Grandad took his hand, nodded to Jan to take the other, and the three began now to climb on the rough grass among the gorse and bracken.

"You know, lad, from up there on Borley, you can see right over to your house," said Grandad.

"Big deal," grumbled Kevin. But all the same, he looked up at the great rock crown above them. Then he said:

"There's someone up there."

Jan looked where the lad pointed, but the sun's rays slanted against her gaze and she was dazzled. She shaded her hand.

"You're seeing things," she said. "There's no one."

"They're gone now," insisted Kev.

"Get off," she teased.

"There was someone on top, spying with glasses."

Grandad looked at Jan.

"Must have been a bird-watcher," said the old man. "Hey, I've had enough, let's get back. I'm out of puff."

As they turned and began to make their way slowly down the slippery turf of the slope, Kevin went ahead, sliding on his bottom. Then he stood up and shouted,

"There's Dad. I can see Dad in the car. Come on."

21

Jan came down from the hill with Grandad and Kevin, in a strange mood. She felt irritated for some reason, as though Dad, by arriving early and Kev, by his jumping eagerness to be in the car and away home, had in some way prevented her from doing something she wanted to do. But what? Had she wanted to talk to Grandad, to ask him something? Were there questions she wanted answering, things that Grandad could tell her? She searched her mind, there were no questions, just an empty space, a void into which irritation, even anger could flow.

Nerves alert, she sensed something different as she got into the car. Well, there was something different about today. Dad hadn't been there and Gran had said nothing. But there was more to it than that. The car rolled onto the downhill road and picked up speed with Kev making engine noises and steering with his fists clutched in front of him. Dad, she thought, was not offering to let her drive today. Indeed he was driving faster than usual.

"Hey, Dad. There was a spy on Borley Top."

"Get away."

"There was. Somebody with binoculars."

"What, looking for missile bases in Warby?"

"Well, you don't know."

"I expect it was a bird-watcher. They usually have field glasses."

The car moved so fast they were on the town road and past the hospital before Jan realised.

"Hey, hold on," she called, "we didn't look out for Mrs Elsom at the bus stop."

Dad shook his head: "Too early. Good half hour before visiting time ends. Can't hang about all that time."

He was in a rush. It was then that Jan grasped what was different – a slight scent, a smell in the car, cigarette smoke, a very faint after smell. Dad never smoked in the car, he said it was too small, made it stuffy. And behind the whiff of cigarette, there was an even fainter scent, something more personal. Before they reached the town, Jan had placed it. Sandra's perfume.

So? So Sandra and Dad had been out in the car. He hadn't been working at home. Why did he have to tell a story like that? Why did he have to tell her anyway? It was his life, wasn't it?

They reached home and she went into the kitchen to make tea. There was the same twofold scent again. So? Sandra had been in their kitchen before. But that was looking after Kev, wasn't it, not looking after . . . Oh give over, she told herself.

She made tea and went upstairs to change. The faint aroma caught up with her on the landing. She changed and hurried down again, determined not to think about it any more. Nor did she. She had plenty of corners in her mind where she could pack thoughts out of sight, like pushing books or clothes into a cupboard and slamming the door. But feelings, with no shape, no name, no label, cannot be stowed away. They live, they lie in wait, ready to surprise. They jog you when you least expect it. They make you do things you didn't intend, things with no connection, no reason behind them.

And that happened two days later. Dad had come home early to see to Kevin, parked the car outside, and later, when Jan hurried in, he had gone out again on foot, with a "See you later." She had paid no attention, but as she and Kev were playing Scrabble in the front room, she half attentive, Kev smart and aggressive, there was a small knock on the front door. It was Mrs Elsom, pale-faced.

For a second, Jan's heart stopped. Was old Joe dead? But it was something more humdrum.

"I've missed me bus, love. Do you think you could ask your Dad if . . .?"

"Oh, he's out."

The old woman was close to tears. Jan took a sudden decision.

"Hang on a sec."

She went back into the house, ran upstairs and looked on Dad's desk. The car keys were there. She snatched them up and ran down.

"Going out, Kev, won't be long."

"Where're you off to?" Kev's face peered round the front room door sharp eyes catching the glint of the key ring in her hand.

"Never you bloody mind."

"Charming."

She slammed the door and put an arm over Mrs Elsom's shoulder.

"Come on, love."

"Oh, do you think you should?"

"Not really," she answered flippantly. "But no one'll know."

The journey, for a marvel, was trouble free. Jan could drive the car and knew it – when she was alone at the wheel. There was not long to wait either, for the old man had taken a turn for the worse that afternoon and lay sedated and snoring in his bed. The sister advised his wife not to wait: "Come back tomorrow, it'll be all right. Give us a ring first though."

They were back in the street in under an hour and Dad was still out. The keys were back on the desk and she back in the front room playing Scrabble when he returned. She greeted him like an innocent, naughty child and went up to her room.

Of course Kevin told his dad when he went to bed, with all the innocent malice of an eight-year-old.

Later, before she went to bed, there was a short, terse exchange of words in the kitchen. Dad used words like irresponsible, please yourself, don't think of others (that hurt), could have been a total disaster, no more driving lessons, big deal.

She said nothing. She could say nothing. But her dark feelings lurked still at the edge of her mind. They had not finished with her yet.

22

At work Jan was at ease, at her best. When the pressure was high her excitement mounted. When she solved some problem her spirits rose. The inner office atmosphere, the contrast of Margaret Hardwick's calm efficiency and David Thompson's energetic, boyish good humour suited her. She was among adults and treated like one. Even Lorraine, more and more sullen, did not bother her and she barely noticed the tension that was rising between that young woman and Penny.

She had her work and her studies. She was moving on. And there was that little treat each week, that carefully casual, discreet trip from the car park, empty in autumn dusk, in David Thompson's car to the little café and the relaxed chat over the large, gold-rimmed coffee cups in the deep armchairs. Then the quiet drive back, always stopping a little way from her street and the quick rush home, under a dark empty sky, with the yellow moon peering over the chimney pots.

"I think you like it here." Margaret Hardwick was looking at her across the desk.

"Oh, I do."

"You've settled in wonderfully well, Jan. I'll be honest, I did not expect you to take to the work. But you have a touch. You could do well provided . . . oh, but you don't want my advice. The thing is, Jan, next month you'll complete the trial period and we'll be talking about a contract and permanent job. I mean, as far as anything can be permanent."

"How do you mean, Miss Hardwick?"

"There are at least two or three bigger firms who might

move in on Cartwright's. It's no longer a family firm. It could be taken over, which might mean anything – expansion or shutdown, just like that."

She snapped her fingers.

"However, one bridge at a time. Next month, for one, you are due for more money. We are getting you on the cheap. Both Da – Mr Thompson and I know that. And we shall see that you get a decent raise. And more important, we must talk about where you are going. You don't want to be a PA for ever."

Jan shrugged: "I don't like to think ahead too much. I'm just getting going and I'm enjoying it."

A curious expression came into Margaret Hardwick's eyes.

"Fair enough. But enjoyment doesn't always last."

She said no more. Jan filed the conversation in her mind. But she kept the thought of more money handy. Now she could begin to buy her own things, like clothes, for real, and at last be herself. If she knew who that was.

She began to look more closely in the shops, bigger, more expensive places like Barker's. She thought about a stylish winter coat and boots.

And two more days passed before the next ambush came.

It happened one lunchtime and it was over and done, not to be prevented nor remedied, before she even realised the part she had played. She was in the works, taking a note from Margaret Hardwick to the Production manager when she ran into Tina Ellis. The line had just stopped and the women were streaming away in all directions, some heading towards school, or child-minder's home, some just heading home for the afternoon, and others to the canteen. Jan walked along amid the crowd, chatting to Tina. She knew she was noticed and eyed by the women as well as the men – Mum's dresses, the way she walked. Ever since Sandra had told her that her long stride gave a swing to her walk, she had tried now and then to shorten her step. But then she had thought – what the hell? Let 'em look, let 'em think. That's their problem, not mine.

Before she knew it, busy with her conversation, she had gone into the canteen with the women and taken her place alongside Tina in the rapidly forming queue. Over her shoulder she saw some of the men from Maintenance – Tina's father, Darren Porter. They nodded. The queue moved on. Jan turned away, tray in hand to speak to the service lady. But instead she found herself face to face with Miss Baldwin, the manageress. The little black eyes were bright with menace.

"Have we changed our job again?"

Jan stared and almost looked to one side as if someone else were being addressed. But she knew. Shaking her head she determined not to answer too quickly.

"Don't you think you ought to be on the staff side, Miss Whitfield?"

The voice rose slightly, stilling the chatter in the queue, gathering a slightly intimidating crowd, an audience. Even the serving ladies paused, ladles in hand. There was an air of expectancy. A little row was in the making.

Jan kept calm: "As it happens I'm having my lunch here with a friend and I don't think it really causes you any bother if I do."

"Oh does it not?" The voice went a fraction higher, drawing in more listeners, increasing the area of silence. "And is it no bother for the staff people if all your friends from the works come over on your side?"

Jan picked up her plate, half turning towards the table. She could feel the anger rise inside her. She wouldn't say any more. But she did, fatally.

"I don't think there's any point in falling out over it."

"I'm sure you don't. No point, if you're in the wrong."

Now Miss Baldwin turned and began to move towards the kitchen. The conversation began again, but in lowered tones. But in the bare second's silence before it rose, Ellis was heard, quietly, but with clear intent to be heard.

"You know what she wants?"

The rest of the sentence was lost as the manageress turned like a fencer and lunged at the counter, coming within a foot of Ellis's face.

"I heard that, Bill Ellis. If you think I am going to . . ."

"Oh, give over." Ellis's voice was calm and brutal. "I wasn't talking to you. I was chatting to my mates. You know what they say about people who listen in?"

"Don't you give me that. You used a filthy word and you did it to insult me. And I've had enough of people like you."

"What d'you mean – people like me?"

"You know what I mean. Men!" The word was spat out. "Well, this time you have overstepped the mark. Either you take that back or . . ."

"Or what?"

"I go straight upstairs about it." The manageress gestured towards the Admin block. Then she spoke to the queue:

"You all heard what he said."

There was an uncomfortable stir, then silence. The manageress's lips tightened.

"Very well." She turned to her assistants. "You carry on here."

Without another word, she moved to the counter, lifted the flap and stepped out. The queue parted·like magic to make way. Then the serving began again and the line moved forward as she disappeared through the dining room door.

As Jan entered the office again after lunch she found Margaret Hardwick and David Thompson talking together. They turned as she came in.

"Well, Jan," said Margaret, "just what happened down there today?"

Uncomfortably Jan went over the story. Margaret Hardwick shook her head.

"I was afraid we might have trouble if you went in for lunch on the other side again, Jan. I thought you'd realised. It isn't worth having a row over."

"Oh come on, Margaret." David Thompson spoke so quickly that both women looked at him in surprise.

"I'm sorry. But Jan going to lunch on the works side has very little to do with it. Miss Baldwin has been spoiling for a fight with someone for months now. That is the third time she has made a complaint this year. You know that."

Margaret Hardwick's colour heightened. "That may be so. But no one should be allowed to get away with obscene abuse like that. And William Ellis is loud-mouthed and foul-mouthed, and it is not the first time that he has caused trouble either."

David Thompson shrugged:

"Obscenity? Just an old Anglo-Saxon word – shafted." He looked quickly from one to the other.

"David!" Margaret Hardwick's voice was level. "The meaning is absolutely clear and absolutely unacceptable. The very least he could do is take it back."

David Thompson made a face. "Knowing Ellis, that is not very likely. Anyway," he turned towards his office, "it's out of our hands now, she's gone right up to the boss, threatened to resign, to sue. We'll just have to wait and see."

As the afternoon passed so the rumours began to fly through the building from floor to floor. Ellis wouldn't apologise. Miss Baldwin had told Livermore that either he did or else . . . Then Livermore had told Ellis, through Norris Cooper, that either he took the word back or he'd be off the works by Friday. And Darren Porter had been up and now there was talk of a strike. The whole works was alive with whispered information, speculation about how far the affair would go and disputes about its rights and wrongs.

Two groups quickly formed. Neither Ellis nor Miss Baldwin had many friends and all agreed it was a stupid matter to shut the works down over. The thing was who should give way? Down in the works the women argued as they picked and sorted on the moving line. Some said: "He ought to go, he's a menace." But those nearest Tina reckoned that Miss Baldwin was a spiteful cow and the way she spoke to people would make a saint swear.

"All the same," said both groups, "do you think they'll shut down?"

"Expect so. Gone too far now. Ah well, get on, girls, we'll be sitting on our hands come Friday."

The chattering groups grew silent as Jan passed, then talk began again. She knew they were talking about her. Back at her desk she fiddled with her papers as the afternoon crawled by. Her heart grew heavier. Margaret Hardwick and David Thompson disappeared upstairs to meetings in Livermore's office. Around five, David Thompson suddenly looked in.

"Better go on home, Jan. This is going to be a long one."

He looked at her, then suddenly came forward and touched her cheek lightly with his fingers.

"Cheer up, Jan. This has absolutely nothing to do with you. This one has been brewing up for months. It was bound to come. You were just in the way when the flak started to fly. See you tomorrow."

23

There was no escape from the excitement at Cartwright's even in college. Next morning Jan found the dispute was already under discussion. At the cafeteria tables, students in her group demanded to know:

"Hey, Jan, you work at Cartwright's, don't you? Is it right there's going to be a shutdown because a bloke said a rude word to a bird?"

"That was no bird, that was an old broiler," called someone further along the table.

"Typical," snapped one of the girls. "You blokes are all the same. Can't open your mouths without being insulting."

Jan shook her head.

"How do you lot know about it? It only happened yesterday lunchtime."

They laughed: "Don't you read the daily papers?"

"Not the ones you lot read," she retorted. "Anyway," she hesitated uncertain of how much to say, "if there's a strike, it'll be over a bloke being sacked, not over a word."

"Same difference. But why all the fuss? Folk are using naughty words all the time. Why shut a factory down over one?"

"It's worse," said one student quietly, "when a bloke says things like that to a woman."

"What did he say?" They looked at Jan. "The papers didn't say."

"The *Sun* did," added one.

"Yeah. I bet they got it wrong. Go on, Jan."

She looked at them, uncertain. She saw again the outraged face, the snapping eyes of the manageress, the brutal contempt in Ellis's eyes.

"You know what she wants – a bloody good shafting."

The table rocked with laughter. Then there was silence as a girl spoke.

"That proves my point. You blokes just think it's funny, don't you? Well, it's not."

"Sure, it's insulting. But sticks and stones will break my bones – names'll never hurt me."

"That's what you think. But what was he talking about, eh? He was talking about rape, wasn't he?"

"How do you make that out?"

"Well, I can't imagine the woman fancied him, can you?"

"Well, you know what they say about women getting past it. They get a bit desperate like."

"Can't you get it into your head that every woman isn't gasping to be screwed by every bloke," she hesitated, as if embarrassed by the strength of her feelings, "not all the time."

The laughter was quieter now and one of the men tried to change the subject. He turned to Jan.

"It's a bit unusual, I mean for management to be so smart at it, I mean giving him the heave so quickly."

She shrugged. "Well, there's ninety per cent women at Cartwright's. Maybe that's it."

But, maybe it wasn't. She came back into the office towards the end of lunchtime and as she passed the half-open door of the tech room she heard voices, Lorraine's and another. It wasn't Penny and they were speaking in excited half whispers. She was about to go in when she realised that the second talker was Vikki Cooper. She made a quick decision, moved quietly on into Margaret Hardwick's room, and there, with equal quietness opened the side door a half inch and sat down at the desk as if working. Now she could hear the voices.

"Well, they're in for a shock this time, Mr William Ellis and his mates."

"Go on."

"Well, we're going to let 'em go out on strike."

"Let 'em?"

"Yes, my Norris was in with Henry Livermore – just the two. So this musn't go any further."

"Promise, but I don't get it, why should they let the place shut down like that, just for one bad word?"

Vikki Cooper sniggered: "Do you think he gives a damn about Madam Baldwin, that old bag, and her feelings? If he had his way, he'd have her out as soon as wink, and close the canteen as well. It's losing money."

Vikki Cooper's voice rose and fell.

"No, we're telling Darren Porter and the blokes – here's the line, one foot over and you're out.'

Jan smiled at Vikki Cooper's "we".

"Seems a bit risky, doesn't it?"

"Not a bit. Listen. You know when the blokes come out the women get paid for lost time. Right?"

"Right."

"Well, this time, we won't. He's been waiting for a chance to get rid of that stupid business for years. He'll just lay 'em off and close it all down. Orders are slackening off at the moment so no problem. Then, it's down to the women. If they want their pay, they can tell the blokes to go back to work."

"That's drastic."

"I know. That's why they've been at it so long upstairs. Thompson and Hardwick reckon it's breaking an agreement and we'll have the national unions on our necks. They say there should have been an inquiry before Ellis was sacked. If the unions went to the tribunal, Cartwright's might have to pay damages."

There was a pause for effect, then, "You know what Henry Livermore said to David Thompson? 'Who's running this place, David, me or Darren Porter?'"

"Ooh."

"He doesn't care if it goes on till Christmas. In fact round about Christmas is when the silly cows in Production'll feel it most."

There was a movement in the outer office, a chair pushed back.

"I must dash."

"Yes, Penny Castle'll be here in a minute."

"Right, now not a word to her. You know what she's like about unions. And especially not a word to madam in there."

Madam. That's me, thought Jan.

"She's bound to know, isn't she?"

"I should coco. Thompson and all the other managers have had to agree not to say a word. If it gets out, if they call off the strike and go to the tribunal, well, my dear boss will be very, very peeved. So, think on it."

"Cross my heart."

Now the other room was silent, Jan cautiously opened the door. The two had gone. She sat down on the top of her old desk and tried to grasp the full meaning of what she had heard. She was still there when Penny came bustling in.

"Hello, Jan," she said, cheeks pink with excitement. "It looks as though the blokes are going to walk out. And it won't be a one day wonder, either. This is for real."

She looked at Jan's face reading something there.

"Look, Jan, I know Tina's dad had no right to say that to Miss Baldwin, but Cartwright's have no right just to give him the push, not without looking into it. It's almost as if they wanted a showdown."

"They do," said Jan

Penny stared: "Are you serious?"

Jan nodded. She told Penny quickly what she had overheard. Penny's hand went to her mouth.

"What a cow she is, that Vikki Cooper. She just hates the unions."

"That's not the point," said Jan. "Point is, what about the women in the works. How are they going to be fixed, no money, seven or eight weeks to Christmas? Listen, do you think Darren and the blokes realise this?"

Penny shook her head.

"Don't think they can. There'd be such a bust-up between the women and the blokes, and all over bloody Bill Ellis."

She put her hand on Jan's arm.

"Listen. I'm going to tell Darren."

Jan looked at Penny's amiable face, drawn and tight-lipped.

"If they find out you've done that, Penny, you'll be for the high jump. You can't afford that."

"I don't give a . . ." Penny's voice shot up the scale, then she put a hand to her mouth. She walked smartly across the room and closed the door to the corridor.

"I know what I'll do, Jan. I trust you. I am going to go to Darren Porter's tonight after work. He lives near us. I'm going to tell him. That way no one knows how he found out."

"They could guess."

"Guessing's one thing, proving's another."

She touched Jan's arm again.

"Thanks, Jan. You'd better make sure they don't find out you told me."

Jan shrugged: "Nobody told me anything."

24

On Friday the word spread round the firm. The strike was off, or postponed. Union officials from outside were coming in and there were more talks. The lifts in the Admin block were busy with men in raincoats and brief-cases. David Thompson and Margaret Hardwick were upstairs. Secretaries rushed to and fro with sandwiches and coffee. Jan was left on her own. Penny and Lorraine sat silently in the other office and Jan left them alone. She carefully chose a different time from Penny to go to lunch and, of course, stayed on the staff side. But there was no sign of the manageress. The word was that both she and Ellis had been sent home on full pay. Everything was happening, nothing was happening. No one knew for sure.

Towards the end of the afternoon, Jan made ready to go home. There was no sign of her boss coming down. Next door she heard Penny and Caroline go off line and leave the office. Jan stayed on, idly turning the pages of a text-book, *Personnel Management and the Handling of Disputes*. She was tired, it made no sense to her, procedure, rules. Did she want to spend her life involved in things like that? To her there were rights and wrongs and if it were wrong how could it be the rule? You just did something about it – if you could. So she had not hesitated in telling Penny what she had overheard. Whether it was a good idea in the long run, she was not sure. But about whether it was right or not, she was quite sure.

"I wouldn't wait on if I were you, Jan."

Margaret Hardwick had returned and was clearing her desk. "I expect Mr Thompson will be a little while. But I think it's all over for today. I'm off home."

Jan fiddled with her papers while the other woman snapped shut her briefcase.

"I've just one or two bits to finish off."

"Suit yourself." Margaret Hardwick paused in the open doorway. "Don't overdo things though."

That was a funny way of putting it, thought Jan, as the door closed. Or was it? Am I getting suspicious? She knew she felt guilty about what she had done behind Margaret's back. And she knew she was pretending to work when she just wanted to wait until David came down, in case . . . So maybe she was reading too much into innocent words.

Outside dusk closed in. The room faced east, and a line of trees in the distance caught the last rays of the sun and glowed pink, their bare branches standing out against a paling sky.

David Thompson was suddenly in the room, by her desk.

"Still here, Jan? Good." He paused and looked at her. "No, not more work. I need a drink, and I mean a drink drink. Like to – join me?"

She was on her feet, stuffing book and papers into her bag, in comic haste and not bothering to conceal her eagerness, childishly afraid he might vanish through the door before she was ready. But he was standing there, coat over his shoulders, watching her with a smile.

"OK?"

As they went down the silent corridors to the car park they knocked slightly against one another, shoulders, arms touching. He steadied her, put a hand under her elbow, then outside, the hand was slipped through her arm, until they reached the car.

Once in their seats, he pushed the door slightly back cutting off the courtesy light, then leaned over and kissed her. She caught her breath and was glad of the darkness inside the car.

"You looked as tired as I feel," he said.

She said nothing. She did not trust her voice. If she spoke, she knew her voice would squeak.

He started the engine, and as they drove out, let his breath go in a whistle.

"Well, it's over. Both suspended on full pay pending the inquiry. Then I expect compensation and please don't come back. Not ideal – but."

He turned a corner strongly, throwing her against him for a second.

"Still a bloody sight better and cheaper for everyone than a full scale dispute."

He pulled up outside a quiet pub across town. The saloon bar was empty save for two regulars chatting to the barmaid. They sat down in a corner by an open fire. He looked at her.

"Tonic please," she said.

"Sure?"

"Sure."

"Suit yourself, I need something stronger."

When he returned with the drinks he sat down next to her and took a deep pull at his glass.

"I needed that. Two, three days of cardboard sandwiches and plastic coffee are enough to ruin the stomach lining."

He looked ahead, speaking as if to himself.

"Funny how the atmosphere suddenly changed today. Strike called off, people in from outside asking awkward questions. Mind you, I'm not grumbling, though the boss wasn't too pleased."

"Oh, why?" Jan made herself ask. Why was he gossiping to her like this? The guilt feelings awoke in her mind.

"He thinks someone tipped the unions off. You know, a leak like they have in Downing Street."

He looked at her.

"Someone in one of the offices, they reckon, but who? You haven't any idea . . .?"

Then he stopped, squeezed her arm and said:

"Give over, Thompson. Ask a nice girl out for a drink, then talk shop. Sorry, Jan."

He looked at her again.

"Have I told you how great you look in that outfit?"

"No, but you can do."

He laughed. "That's better." They both relaxed and chatted about other things, as they always did, so comfortably when they were alone.

"Another, Jan?"

She ought to be on her way really, but – oh sod the glass slipper. Yes please.

He was on his way to the bar before she had even voiced the thought. She sat still, enjoying the warmth of the fire and the quiet peaceful feeling inside her. She stood up to loosen her coat.

"Hello, Jan."

The familiar voice came from her left and it warned her before she identified it. Instinctively, she stopped, hand on button, as if she were doing her coat up. Just a couple of yards away, about to sit down at a nearby table, were Peter Carey and Sharon. Of all the coincidences, ex-boyfriend, ex-girlfriend, turning up when she was with David.

"Alone, Jan?" Sharon smiled sweetly. "We saw you as we came in.' I said, 'Look, Peter, look who's here? Jan Whitfield.'"

Jan made herself look at them. Sharon smiled but her eyes were cool and calculating. Peter Carey was not smiling, but his eyes were friendly. This was Sharon's idea, she knew. Pete hadn't wanted to come over but Sharon could just not resist rubbing it in. See how you blew it, Jan dear? Pete's with me now.

Was she on her own? David Thompson had always been so discreet going into the car park when everyone else had left, finding the quiet café, dropping her off a little way from home. In the office he was correct, though friendly.

What should she say? She glanced quickly at the table in front of her.

There were no glasses, no telltale signs of a PA out with her boss. Then a quick glance at the bar, and her heart gave a painful knock. David had gone, just disappeared. Ah well.

She made a would-be friendly face at Sharon.

"Having a bit of a breather before going home."

"Bit out of your way? We're here because Pete works round the corner now, at Peak Radio."

She was waiting for Jan to react, but Jan ignored it.

"It's quiet here. I like it." Jan was cool, but thought to herself – liar, never been here before.

The barmaid was at her elbow.

"One tonic, dear."

"Room service eh?" Sharon quipped. Jan smiled, looked at them, and sat down. Pete's gaze was level. She had a feeling he might smile if they were alone. But maybe that was her fancy. Probably he wouldn't be here if they were on their own. That was daft.

"It was my idea to come over. Pete didn't want to," rubbing it in, "but now that he's reporting for Peak Radio (hear that, Whitfield) I thought you might be able to give him a rundown on the dispute at Cartwright's."

There was a split-second movement from Peter Carey, half a lift of the eye, quarter turn of the head. It said louder than words, forget it, it wasn't my idea.

She drank her tonic and stood up.

"Dispute's off. I should think it's all over town by now. Just boring old talks. No story. In any case, I'm just an office girl."

She buttoned her coat, Pete spoke at last.

"Thanks. See you around."

That shut Sharon up all right.

"See you."

She went out through the saloon bar door, and the cold clear air hit her. David Thompson's car had gone.

It seemed a long walk home.

That night she slept restlessly, turning and waking time after time. Towards dawn she fell asleep and dreamt a vivid dream. She was walking alone on the slopes of Borley Top. Far above her sat a lone figure, eyes turning to sweep the landscape, but not looking at Jan. Jan began to climb faster, more breathlessly, but as she climbed, so the figure moved away, always too far in front for Jan to see the face.

But she knew who it was. When she woke in the morning, she found her cheeks were wet.

25

Depression and anger did battle inside Jan's mind at the weekend. David Thompson had walked out on her without a word or even a hasty signal from the door of the pub. It shocked her and made her feel foolish all at once. All right, he wanted to be discreet in his personal life. But what was wrong with being seen in a pub together on the other side of town?

This and the appearance of Peter Carey made the whole business almost humiliating. She had not been face to face with Peter since the early summer when their affair had come to a sudden, noisy end. She had shouted, he had fled. Not that he had anything to say for himself now, Sharon had seen to that. The meeting had been arranged by her, just to let Jan know – you're out, I'm in. Why did women have to play these stupid games? But what was going on in Pete's mind as he sat there between them, current girlfriend, and ex-girlfriend. Jan had a suspicion he wished himself a mile away. Sharon was remorseless. Of course she had been sweet and biddable which Jan hadn't. But now Sharon wanted her investment back with interest. Still that was Mr Carey's problem now, wasn't it? Jan had her own problems – like falling for her boss with just a few kind words, a coffee, a tonic and a quick kiss in a dark car.

She tried to put these thoughts out of her mind by charging through the housework, turning the house upside down, disturbing her father and brother satisfyingly, then feeling ashamed of herself, putting in time in the kitchen to make a Sunday lunch with apple crumble just like Warby Gran made. Amazing how it sweetened everyone.

In the afternoon Dad went to his room to work, while she played Monopoly with Kev. The little devil won and was highly delighted with himself. Then she decided her good deeds were done for the weekend and she took herself off for a long walk. The setting sun was low and red, the top branches of trees stood out bare and thin above the autumn colours of unshed leaves. She remembered suddenly that this week the clocks went forward, or was it back? She had never given a thought to things like this in the past, but then she hadn't thought about apple crumble and chops from the butcher's, and have we got toilet paper and sugar in the house and has Kev got a clean pair of pants for school on Monday? That had all been taken care of and Jan had just thought about Jan and that was enough to be going on with. That made her think about David Thompson again. Her heart sank. She shivered. It was growing dark and the moon was coming up on the other side of the river. She turned and went home.

On Monday she came in to work late and found that if she had forgotten the dispute, other people had not. She heard voices raised as she came down the passage. Three voices, two against one and very unpleasant. In the tech room Penny stood with her back to the fax table.

Face pale, hair was falling over her eyes, but thrown back every few seconds as she spoke. Just inside the doorway was Vikki Cooper, pointing a finger at Penny, voice sharp and brittle. Leaning against her desk, putting in a word or two now and then, was Lorraine.

"It must have been you," Jan was almost at Vikki Cooper's side and saw her in profile, the sharp line of nose and mouth, the flick of eyelash. "You're the only one who's in the union in the office."

"Right," added Lorraine, "and I'll tell you something else. She lives in the same road as Darren Porter. She must have gone straight down there on Thursday night and tipped him off."

Jan stepped into the room. There was a sudden silence. She looked from one to the other. No point in being quiet about it.

"What's all this?" she demanded.

Vikki Cooper breathed in and put on her top office voice.

"Someone gave the unions confidential information about management. Mr Livermore is very angry."

Jan looked at her calmly. She could sense Penny's nervousness increase now that she was in the room.

"What's the fuss? The strike's off. Everybody should be smiling."

"That is not the point." Vikki Cooper's voice took on a faintly pompous note. "When the union officials came in from outside, they had information about what management intended to do. Someone on the staff side must have passed it on to them."

She turned her back on Jan and spoke to Penny:

"Can you deny you went and spoke to Darren Porter?"

Penny looked at Jan. Jan could feel her distress.

"It's nothing to do with you what I did."

"Oh, you can't deny it then." She moved towards Penny. "Right, you can come up to Mr Livermore's office and tell him all about it."

"I'm not doing anything of the sort. You've no right."

Penny was defiant but close to tears.

Vikki Turner smiled unpleasantly.

"In that case, I shall go upstairs myself and report to him and we'll see what happens."

"Hang about," Jan's voice was harsh. She was amazed at her own coolness. "I'll come up with you, Vikki."

"What d'you mean? What's it got to do with you?"

"One thing at a time, Mrs Cooper." Jan had been about to say Madam but switched on the instant, and knew that Vikki Cooper knew. "Answer me one thing."

Vikki stared but said nothing.

"If Penny told Darren Porter what Mr Livermore was up to, who told her? Mr Livermore doesn't share his secrets with her, does he?"

"How should I know?" Vikki Cooper's voice shrank.

Jan took half a step forward. The heat in her was rising through the cool. "I will tell you how she knew. Because you came down here on Thursday, at lunchtime, and passed the confidential bits on to your little friend Lorraine."

"She never," began Lorraine, then "how did . . .?"

"You might well ask. I'll tell you. I was in there next door and heard the lot. So there were three people who knew. If Penny found out it's because one of us told her."

"It was you then." Vikki Cooper's eyes sparked. "You've always been very friendly with Ellis and Porter, haven't you?"

It was Jan's turn to smile unpleasantly.

"I might have been. I do happen to think that it was a dirty trick to stop the women's pay." She snorted: "Big deal, eh. Lady gets insulted by man, so management stops the women's pay – to punish the men, I suppose. Great stuff."

"It must of been you," said Lorraine, her genteel speech fraying.

Jan turned on her so suddenly that Lorraine winced. "I'll tell you something, Miss. Neither you nor Vikki can prove that Penny or I talked to the union. But we all know who leaked the confidential stuff in the first place, don't we?"

She pushed closer to Vikki Cooper.

"So, come on, Vikki love, let's all go up the wooden hill to Mr Livermore, and tell him everything like good little girls. Never mind Penny. You tell Mr Livermore how you went straight down from his room and told it all to Lorraine, and I'll tell him how I eavesdropped on you.

Then we'll both burst into tears and promise never to do it again."

Vikki hesitated a second, speechless. Jan grabbed her wrist.

"What are you waiting for? Come on."

"Jan, what is this?"

All four started, Margaret Hardwick stood in the doorway. "I could hear you shouting down the corridor."

Vikki Cooper was swift to sense rescue. She moved to leave the room.

"I'm sorry, Margaret. We were just having a little argument about something unimportant and I'm afraid Jan forgot herself." She stepped past Margaret Hardwick into the passage. "Nothing of any importance."

Jan looked quietly at her boss.

"That's right, nothing that need go any further, eh Vikki?"

Vikki nodded and disappeared. Penny's face collapsed into a silly smile.

"Funny how a big row will blow up about something quite ridiculous," she said.

Lorraine said nothing but went to her desk. Margaret Hardwick beckoned Jan through into the inner office, shut the door, looked at her a moment and shook her head.

"Well, I know what that was all about. But I don't want to know. Promise me one thing, Jan. In future, be careful. You are a very courageous young woman, you have a great sense of right and wrong. But you are reckless, too impulsive for your own good. Try to think things through a little more, or ask for a second opinion. You know you can talk to me. Now," she went on more briskly, "Mr Thompson is away for a few days – on a course. But I understand he came in yesterday and has left work for you. And of course," she smiled, "if you find yourself at a loose end, I can always find you something."

Halfway through the morning the phone rang. Margaret Hardwick turned to Jan.

"Miss Baldwin is coming in to see me. I'll talk to her in Mr Thompson's room. Please show her in when she arrives."

Half an hour later, the canteen manageress swept into the office. Jan held the door of David Thompson's office open for her, but Miss Baldwin neither looked at her nor spoke. Jan shrugged and went back to her work. But a little later when that lady came out and passed her desk again, Jan got up and spoke to her.

"Miss Baldwin."

The older woman stopped and looked at her coldly.

"I wanted to say I'm sorry about what happened. I suppose in a way I started it all off."

Miss Baldwin sniffed, made as if to leave, then stopped and came back to stand at Jan's desk.

"I suppose you are sorry," she said slowly. "I suppose you're really quite nice underneath. Your mother was a nice person."

She shifted her handbag under her arm.

"In fact, it made no difference what you did. It was bound to happen somewhen, with that mob on the works. Huh, they think I'm a snob, maybe I am. I don't join in with them. Why do they expect everyone to be like them? Live and let live, they say. But they mean live like us and we'll leave you alone. I deal straight, they don't. They hate me and I despise them. I have been expecting trouble with that pig Ellis for a long time. Men are all the same, think they're lords of creation, do what they like and we have to put up with it. Well, I don't."

She stared at Jan.

"Don't get me wrong. I'm not a feminist. I don't think every woman's my sister. If you knew my sister. But I'll tell you this. Men need women. They can't manage without them. But women don't need men. I've managed

131

without them all right and never missed them. Well, I don't suppose we shall see one another again. They're paying me off, and I can't say I'm sorry. I knew they'd get rid of me some day, and half the women in production as well when the time comes – you'll see."

She paused in the door.

"You'll be all right, I expect. They always seem to need secretaries. But just watch out for yourself. I know girls your age have no sense of shame, so I won't say you ought to be ashamed of yourself, but you ought to know better for your own good. You know what I mean, Miss, my stock-room overlooks the car park. You're not the only one who works late. And don't think he'll risk his job just for the sake of your lovely eyes. I'll say no more – goodbye."

The door closed. Jan sat, dumbstruck. It was some little while before she could concentrate on her work again.

But after lunch she forgot the conversation completely. She went into David Thompson's room and found the file waiting for her which he had left the day before. As she turned the papers over she found a little sealed envelope. On the outside were two words in light pencil – "Velly solly".

She opened the envelope, read the few words inside and then got on with her work at her own desk in the other room.

After a while Margaret Hardwick looked up and said:

"Jan, do you mind not whistling like that? It's a bit too hearty for me."

26

On Saturday morning, Jan had her hair cut shorter so that it curled round ears and neck. She made lunch for Dad and Kev and put it in the oven, then got out the green dress. Dad looked at her as she walked down the stairs. He seemed about to say something, but then changed his mind.

Kev said:

"You're going out with a feller."

"Brilliant, Sherlock," she answered flippantly. She looked over at Dad.

"I'll be back at teatime, Dad."

Then she was away. She walked through the parade and David picked her up in one of the side streets. He put an arm round her shoulder and squeezed gently.

"You look great."

She felt great.

They spoke no more while he manoeuvred the car through the shopping traffic then clear of the town and away to the open country on the north east side. It was a glorious day, a gentle warmth, a clear sky, the sun glowing and a sleepy calm in the air, like the last farewell of the Indian summer.

The road wound upwards in a direction Jan was unfamiliar with. As fields and hedges gave way to stone walls and rough pastures, David lowered the window and let the soft air fill the car. The radio played quietly, music Jan did not recognise, but she liked it. Everything was right today. At the top of a rise, he pulled into the side and stopped the car. Behind them they looked down on the town, in front the patchwork fields of another valley with villages, an occasional farm or factory, and beyond more hills, gentle brown and green in the sun. There was a distant, subdued sound of birds talking rather than singing to themselves.

David looked at her: "I don't know what to say to you, Jan."

"Well, say nothing then." His embarrassment made her feel older, more in charge. She leaned across and kissed him.

"I panicked that night in the pub. When I went to the bar I looked back and saw that couple come over to you. I asked the barmaid if she knew them and she said the young bloke worked for local radio."

Jan chuckled: "Peter Carey. He's just started there. He left school the same time as me."

"Oh."

What did, "Oh" mean? She went on casually: "We were friends. He's going out with Sharon now, the girl who was there. She wanted to talk about the strike. He didn't. When I looked round, you'd vanished."

His look of embarrassment deepened.

"That's right. With all the kefuffle about the dispute, the last thing I wanted was a chat with a reporter. So I just cleared out. And I forgot I was going to be away. I thought should I ring your home, then I thought better of that. So, I decided to take a chance and write you a note."

"I'm glad you did, David. It's a lovely day and it was kind of you to invite me out for lunch, by way of apology."

"Apology?" he laughed. "Excuse."

She smiled to herself.

They had lunch at a biggish country hotel set back from the road at the end of the valley, under the slope of a hill. They ate in one of the small rooms with only a few tables. It was quiet, only an old, rather posh couple sat at a table in the corner, talking in whispers. The meal was well cooked, but straightforward. She guessed he had planned it this way to put her at ease. There was wine. It was deceptively light. She talked and laughed. She realised this was the first meal she'd had out of work which she hadn't cooked herself, if you left out Gran's at Warby.

Through a side door they looked into another larger room with a big central table. It seemed to be full of girls in red jackets and white blouses, most of them in their twenties, with a sprinkling of older women. There was a buzz of laughter and chat, but Jan could see no wine on the table, only jugs of orange juice. The chatter died down and one of the older women spoke briefly. Jan paid little attention to this. Then with a scrape of chair legs all got up and the larger room emptied and became quiet.

David grinned: "There's discipline for you, forty-five minutes for lunch and no more."

"Who were they – Butlins or something?" asked Jan.

He laughed: "Oh Jan, those are trainee junior management for Bomex, on a course. Getting the togetherness feeling with a touch of the whip as well."

"Bomex? Isn't that the one that's thinking of buying up Cartwright's?"

His eyebrows went up.

"How did you know that?"

She shrugged. "Oh, you hear all sorts of rumours at college. You know how people talk. Doesn't mean anything. One of these outfits that buy up places and close them down, isn't it just like that?"

"Oh, that's a bit exaggerated, Jan. They cut out dead wood. But they look after the people they employ."

"If they employ 'em you mean?"

He gazed at her a moment, eyes troubled.

"You're a funny girl, Jan," he said at last and reached out to take her hand.

"Laugh a minute me." She felt light-headed. Her fingers touched his palm and without thinking stroked her nails

135

across it gently. He reached for his wine, but did not let go of her hand.

"Let's go for a stroll," he said at last.

"Thought you'd never ask."

"Always joking, Jan?"

She looked down at the table, then at him.

"Do you think I'm daft, really?"

"Oh no, Jan. I think you are anything but daft. I think you are very intelligent, very able and you've got guts. I heard how you saw off Vikki Cooper."

She gaped at him. He smiled.

"Miss Hardwick – Margaret did hear quite a lot of what went on that day, you know. But you don't have to worry. It goes no further. Vikki Cooper isn't going to talk for obvious reasons. And just between you and me, Margaret and I happened to disagree with what the boss was going to do. We both thought it was wrong to try and stir up a strike. So you can say, we were relieved."

He stroked her hand.

"But, Jan, that was high risk stuff. You could have landed in deep water. I would not have wanted that. Working with you has been . . ."

He stopped as the waiter came in with the bill.

Outside the sun stood overhead and the air had warmed so much that they walked with coats over their arms. As they strolled up the narrow road behind the hotel he took her hand again and they grinned at one another. They climbed a stile and took a path up the hill. He put an arm round her waist and she leant so that her head rested on his shoulder. Then they stumbled on the rough grass and held hands again.

There was a lazy, drowsy emptiness in Jan's head as they moved up the hill, swaying this way and that. The warm autumn air seemed to invade every part of her body. They leaned into one another. He stopped and kissed her, a long kiss which travelled deep down. She put her hands on his shoulders and felt the muscles through the shirt.

"Hey, there's someone up there watching us."

He turned, suddenly looking where she pointed, then shook his head.

"Miles away. Probably not looking at us anyway."

But he took her arm and led the way behind a small spinney in a hollow below a group of rocks. He threw his coat onto the short, soft turf. She let her coat drop too and sat down. Below them the valley spread out, the hotel appearing no bigger than a cottage at this distance. Beyond were further slopes and in the far distance the shape of the town in the hazy sunshine. Dad and Kev were down there, weren't they? What were they doing now? Oh, what the hell did it matter what anyone's doing now? I'm here, David's here and . . .

They lay now close and kissed. She felt the whole length of his body against hers and sensed his excitement through her own. She was aware vaguely of hands inside her clothes, very gentle and of the flood of feeling they released over the whole surface of her skin. She felt the breeze on her bare thighs. Their tongues mingled, then he shifted his whole body and reached down hers. She gasped,

"David."

"Val," he answered.

She heard the word with some inner ear and only later could she spell it out for her conscious understanding. But she had pulled away from him and tugged down her dress and sat up.

"Sorry, David."

"OK, love." His voice was unsteady.

Now they were on their feet again, smoothing down clothes, picking up coats and walking down the hill. Nothing more was said. That one word had been enough for both. He looked at her as if he wanted to speak but could not bring himself to do it. There was nothing to say.

An hour later the car pulled up in the usual place. He looked at her as if he would speak, but she cut across his words.

"Thanks, David. That was a lovely lunch. I'll see you."

Then she closed the car door and walked away, controlling her steps to stop herself from running. She was home before teatime.

Throughout Sunday, she tried to get down to her studies, but knew that she was putting only a part of her mind to it. The other part was going over what had happened on the hill and what it meant. He had begun to make love to her, but in that moment he had not been thinking of her. She had taken Mum's place in yet another way.

At eight o'clock, after it had gone dark, her struggling thoughts had brought her to a conclusion, a decision. She went to her wardrobe and got out the skirt and blouse she had worn to the disco. She looked at herself in the mirror and put out a tongue at the face there. Then she threw on her coat. "Won't be long," she called and ran from the house.

She made her way swiftly through the streets. The air was cold now and misty. There was a whiff of smoke in the air. Some idiots had been letting off fireworks ready for Bonfire Night next week. Tonight, she guessed, there would be frost. She hugged the coat round her and ran on.

She found his place, a second floor flat in an old Victorian house. She stood a moment outside the door then rang the bell. A moment passed, then she rang again. This time the door swung open and he stood there in shirt sleeves, eyes wide.

"It's Jan," she said.

"I know," he answered, and put out a hand to draw her in.

27

As the last of the autumn days melted away, Jan lived in a world whose only other being was David Thompson. It was a large world, full of light, and it was small, secret, hidden away from anyone else.

It was a world for making love, quietly, speedily at the end of the day, leisurely, talkatively on Sunday afternoons and, once, daft and giggling, in the car parked at the head of the valley, with the windows steamed up.

He was capable, kind and gentle and sometimes with surprise she found herself thinking ruefully of Pete and his awkward would-be manliness. David's easiness released her. She was herself with him and surprised him with her passion and directness. He would gaze in amazement as she strode naked across the carpet in his small flat, making hopscotch steps, then turning to ask:

"What are you gawping at?"

Then, hurling herself on him to wrestle and tickle him, and demand provocatively: "Aren't you ashamed of yourself, seducing your PA?"

And he would answer:

"I didn't. You seduced me. You broke down my resistance."

She would remember that – afterwards.

Or she would sit on his lap, eating chocolates and listening to his music, thinking there were so many things she would like to know about.

In this world she was grand and reckless. She blew all her savings, every last penny on two new outfits, and put Mum's dresses away.

And she was cunning in concealment. No more meetings

in the car park in full view of the canteen storeroom. She walked from work to a street near the parade and leapt into his car, like a taxi. When she visited him in the evenings, she was home early.

In the office she was careful and demure, calling him Mr Thompson and never for one moment letting anyone see what was in her mind. Life was at her fingertips, the world at her feet and she rolled through the days like a kid on skates.

Now there was a second Jan who kept watch outside this world and noticed little things, or saw them, then pushed them skilfully into the back of her mind. She noticed now and then that Margaret Hardwick looked at her as if she were about to say something, a kind of warning frown or purse of the lips, an invisible shake of the head. And it flashed through Jan's mind that Margaret Hardwick might be the teeniest bit jealous, and she had a little giggle about that.

She noticed that Lorraine, sullen and hostile, had given in her notice and that she had not been replaced. Penny, wild-haired and distracted, was doing the work for real. And so Jan would stop now and then, chatting easily and brightly, and give her a hand. And she noticed as she walked through the Production Department that Tina Ellis turned her shoulder so as not to look at her. She shrugged, but that was not so easy to pack away in her mind. It was unfair, wasn't it?

This other Jan noticed other things at home. She came in at a rush with the shopping to find Dad, Sandra and Kev sitting round the kitchen table. And when she said, "Hey, Fatso, hop it, you ought to be in your room," he would put out his tongue and answer impudently. And Sandra would say, "Ah, let him stay a bit." And Dad would add, "Get the other chair out – you know up in my room."

Oh, she knew there was a fourth chair in his room all right.

She would buy in extra sugar, Sandra took two spoonfuls in each cup. Sandra would offer advice on the shopping. "Don't go to Harry's, he's far too pricey. Look, I know a nice butcher, just by the market."

And when she urged Kev off to bed, he would say: "Oh, Sandra lets me watch *Nightwalker*."

And, when she dressed to step out on Sunday afternoons, Dad would say: "Sandra reckons that dress makes you look a bit too old. You're only seventeen you know, love."

Seventeen. That was true, wasn't it? And when she was there amid the three of them, they all made her feel like a schoolgirl again.

And there were, in all this, weekends, bleak times, when David was away, sometimes without warning.

And so there was a third Jan who walked by herself and scuffed her heels through the leaves under the trees, who lay awake at night and stared at the ceiling, or fell asleep and dreamed endless dreams of climbing hills, following someone who had always vanished when she reached the top.

And this Jan noticed one morning as she woke, that the patch of sunlight had moved quite away from her bedroom wall.

Winter

28

There was white frost on the rooftops and pavements when the black car came next door to drive away the wasted body of Joe Elsom to the crematorium.

Jan went to the funeral. Her grey business suit was the closest she could get to mourning, but she found a piece of black velvet ribbon to tie round her neck.

There were a few neighbours, one or two old chaps from the railway and a distant cousin. As they walked into the little chapel with its white pedestal supporting the light brown coffin and its handful of wreaths, Jan felt old Edie Elsom take her arm and hang on tightly. She did not let go until they returned to the house.

A middle-aged man with a tired face, wearing a rumpled grey suit, made a speech. It was short and Jan remembered it, more or less:

"Joe Elsom was a guard for over fifty years. He never kept a train late. They say you could set the station clock by Joe. And he never took promotion, though he knew the system better than most. He had no time for that. What time he had was spent taking up his mates' problems. He was unfashionable, was Joe, in these days. But he was a good man to know."

They sat around with cups of tea and sandwiches in the dark front room. Jan had never been in there. It was cluttered, with old-fashioned furniture, a dining table and high chairs, a long sideboard with pewter dishes and a group of photographs in gilt frames. To Jan's surprise, Mrs Elsom, brown wrinkled face peering oddly from her black dress, suddenly became talkative.

"Yes," she nodded. "It's getting to be a woman's street

this. The blokes have gone, one by one, for this reason or that." She turned to Jan. "Your dad'll soon be the only one left."

"Oh, Edie," said one of the women from the street. "You don't think of your Joe being gone, do you?" She paused and looked round. "I'm sure he's there, watching, you know."

There was a silence as Mrs Elsom shook her head.

"Oh, I don't believe in all that. Neither did Joe. He always said we've got one life. Let's make the most of it."

She rose and carried the teapot round the circle of chairs then stood, holding it like a pointer:

"And another thing he said: 'Don't let 'em bury me, Ede. It's a waste of good ground. Do like we do at the end of the season – a good blaze and finish with it. Then start afresh.'"

There was an uncomfortable silence in the group, but Mrs Elsom had not finished yet:

"Our Joe never believed in," she gestured upwards with the teapot. "Too cold, he reckoned. He promised me that when he went, he'd let me know if there was anything up there. And at the last minute, he looked straight at me and didn't say a thing. He'd have let me know."

She walked into the kitchen with the teapot. The other mourners seemed to take it as a signal to leave. But when she came back she caught Jan's arm and whispered: "Hang on, will you, love?"

Jan went into the hall and brought in the coats, then waited while the others went, one by one, and then helped to clear the plates and cups away.

"Leave those. I'll wash them up later. Plenty of time now."

They went back into the front room.

"Will you draw the curtains, love. I can't reach them without a chair. I'm always afraid of falling off."

The late afternoon light was shut out and the standard

lamp in the corner switched on, bringing a faint gleam of dishes and photograph frames from the sideboard. Jan paused to look: a wedding group, now faded brown, a picture of Joe Elsom in uniform, with the large gun-metal watch in front of it, ticking away, keeping perfect, pointless time.

"I always keep it wound up."

Then a portrait of a baby in old-fashioned bundles of white. Jan stared. She had thought the Elsoms were childless. She had never seen any family come and go. Beside it another picture of a serious young girl in fringe and horn-rimmed spectacles and last of all the same girl, older, in brown uniform and peaked cap. Attached to the corner of the picture was a small multi-coloured ribbon.

"Our Brenda," Mrs Elsom said simply. "In the war."

Then she vanished.

Jan found the old woman in the kitchen, elbows on the table, staring bleakly in front of her. The tears were sliding down the brown weathered cheeks, like rain on dry ground. She bent down and hugged the tiny lean body against her, rocking it like a baby.

"I'm on my own, Jan. On my own. That's where we all end up, isn't it, on our own?"

Jan nodded and rocked silently the old head close to her own.

David was away, and the weekend stretched like a long, white empty road in front of her.

29

On Sunday evening, time and the waiting began to hang heavily on Jan and she ran through the dark streets to David's flat. Perhaps he had come back and she could ease the anxiety that always gripped her when she did not know where he was.

But she was not too impatient. Something held her back from climbing the stairs to ring at his door. Instead she stood on the opposite pavement and looked across at his window. It had begun to rain and the leaves were soggy underfoot. A trick of the light from a street lamp made her believe for a moment that he was home, but it was only a reflection on the window pane. She shivered. Her coat collar was wet to her cheeks but she did not move away until the water dripped from her head and trickled down her face.

In the morning he was away from the office. She got through the day as best she could, working with Margaret Hardwick, answering her questions or remarks with single, tight words, frowning and biting her lip when she thought she was not observed. That night, as soon as she could get away from home she went over to David's place. But there was no sign of him. This time she climbed the stairs, rang the bell and waited, feeling hopeful and foolish and angry with herself at the same time. But there was no answer.

Next day on her desk there was a message from the switchboard. Mr Thompson was back in town but would not be coming in. Would she please carry on as usual. She worked and grew more distracted. The message must mean he was at work in his flat, she thought. Perhaps he was preparing for a board meeting. But he had said nothing to her about this.

The afternoon grew darker, the light went now at half past four. The office lamps came on earlier and made the dark rush up to the windows, enclosing Margaret Hardwick and Jan in a bright square, isolating them from the outside. Jan kept her eyes down on her desk, now and then secretly sliding up her sleeve to check the time. Margaret Hardwick's eyes seemed to be on her, watching each move. At five o'clock the tension brought her to her feet, sliding papers together, all in one movement.

"I've got to get away smartish," she said brightly.

Out came the drawer, in went her papers. The crack of wood meeting wood sounded like a gunshot in the quiet room. She turned to reach for her coat.

"Jan."

She sat down. There was something final about the single, quiet word.

"Don't go, please. Come and sit over here."

Unwilling, childlike, Jan, coat still in her hand, walked across to the other desk and sat down. The older woman leaned over, took the coat from her and hung it up. Then she took a Thermos flask from her bag.

"Cup of coffee, Jan. There's one left and I've had enough."

"I don't know. I was hoping to, like, get away prompt, Miss . . ."

"Jan."

The coffee was poured and passed across the desk.

"I wanted to say something to you. I ought to have said it. But I didn't . . ." Margaret Hardwick paused, "have the nerve. Why, I can't think. Yes, I know what it was – divided loyalties."

She took a deep breath. "No, that's not honest. I was thinking about David Thompson, not about you. I was

149

treating him like a colleague, but not you. I'm sorry, truly."

"I don't understand." But she did, didn't she?

Margaret Hardwick went on. "I was a bit of a coward. I tried hints. You know, woman to woman, that sort of thing, but I could see you thought I was jealous or something like that."

Jan stared. That was true, but how . . .?

Margaret Hardwick read her thoughts. "People in love usually think they are very clever. They think no one else can tell. They think they are invisible. Have you heard of the Arabic proverb: 'There are three things you cannot hide, love, smoke and a man on a camel'?"

Jan gathered her wits.

"I'm not sure it's your business, Miss Hardwick, but, yes, I have been seeing Mr Thompson. But there's no law against that, is there?"

"No, Jan, not illegal. But not legitimate. He's married, Jan, and his wife's just learned she's having a baby. That is where he's been these past few days, home to see her."

Jan knew that in a moment a cold shock would grip her inside and a wave of nausea would sweep up into her head. But not just yet. Her voice was small, like a child's.

"Did he ask you to tell me?"

"No, not directly, though I think he might have hoped I would."

She leaned forward and picked up the empty cup, wiped it and put it away in her bag, then took Jan's hand and pressed it.

"Jan, let me drop you off at home. I won't say any more now. What you do is up to you. But at least you now know."

She moved quickly round the desk and supported Jan as she stood. The walls of the room were slowly revolving. Jan breathed in painfully. The room stood still and they walked out arm in arm.

Once home, she silently made tea for Kev and climbed the stairs to lie down on her bed. The sick numbness gradually left her body and other feelings took over. A sudden shock of embarrassment, of foolishness that made her push her head under the pillow and wish never to leave her room again.

Then she was on her feet, pulling off her clothes in a surge of anger and energy. She changed, threw on her coat, strode into the bathroom splashed water on her face and rubbed it with a towel.

"Where are you off to?"

As usual, little brother watched her. She looked at him. If only he were old enough to mind his own business, or old enough to understand the things he spied on so slyly, old enough to talk to.

"I've got to go out. Won't be long."

"Seeing your boyfriend?"

"Ha ha."

Ha ha. She slammed the front door and clumped off down the street. The rain had gone. In its place was a mean east wind that cut through her clothes. But inside she was warm enough. She could feel the heat grow in her as she walked. Two waves of anger rushed through her body, one for him, one for herself. He for deceiving her, she for kidding herself. But she was angrier with herself. Pride was the strongest part of her and her pride had taken a wounding blow.

There was no light in the window. There was no answer at the door. She stood and banged on it until she heard the door of the flat next door begin to open. Then she fled down the stairs.

The café was empty, no sign of him. There were people in the bar at the pub. They turned round idly as she pushed back the swing doors and then retreated, letting them flap to again.

She went home. Dad was in the kitchen, Kevin was watching the box. She climbed to her room, undressed, went to bed and slept until the light came back to her window. But the sun, of course, had moved away south.

30

By next day the anger with David, with herself, had melted down into something deeper that rested far down in her mind, a feeling rather than a thought, that lay quietly and accusingly, a sense of shame.

Somewhere, she wasn't sure where, was someone, a woman, not all that much older than herself, just about to have a baby, like Mum all those years ago. Someone left to her own life while her husband was away. And that woman did not know that her husband, the man who came home, when he could, and kissed her and got into bed with her, and . . . he was spending his week nights and his Sunday afternoons when he could spare them, with this – girl from the office, a kid really, just out of school.

Or did she know? Had he told her? Had they talked about her? The thought leapt out of hiding and took a stranglehold on her mind, leaving her white-faced and shaken, staring out of the window.

"Jan, dear, would you like to go home?"

Margaret Hardwick was bending over her.

"No, Miss. It's all right."

For a split second, she was back in school with an anxious teacher at her side.

"No, honestly, I'd rather carry on here. I'll feel worse if I stay at home."

Margaret Hardwick nodded.

"That's right. Work's the only cure. Work and other people. I know."

She knew?

Jan worked and put herself in balance again. She chatted with Margaret Hardwick, helped Penny in the tech room, walked the corridors, strode through the Production Department, nodding to people, avoiding Tina Ellis. Work and other people – but not all other people. Not those whose lives you'd helped turn upside down.

And in the evenings she would, without thinking of it, deliberately not thinking of it, she would go home, see to things, change, slip out again and run through the dark and biting streets, head down against the wind. First to his flat, not to ring or knock, or bang on the door and shout and scream outside but just to stand hunched up across the road and see, was it his light, or just the street lamp glinting on the glass. Then to the café, not to drink a miserable solitary cup, but just to look around and walk out again, ignoring the stares of the waitress. Then into the pub bar, through the swing doors and out again. Just a second's glance would tell her who was not there. And now the regulars did not even turn their heads.

She had come to the point where she ran through this evening routine not because she hoped or believed anything but because she did not know how to stop, nor did she dare.

"Jan."

Margaret Hardwick stood by her desk. It was late afternoon. Where had the day gone? What had she done?

"Come and have a drink. I'll drop you off afterwards."

They went to a discreet pub in quite another part of town, the posher part, up the hill. The lounge was small and quiet and warm, like the sitting room of a largish house.

"I live just up the road. You'll have to come and see it sometime. Like to?"

Jan nodded and waited for another blow to fall.

"Jan, I'm afraid I owe you another apology. I didn't tell you the whole story."

Silence. Jan could see the clock hand over the fireplace tick the seconds away.

"David (no Mr Thompson now) won't be coming back to Cartwright's."

She looked at Jan's stricken face and went on hurriedly.

"He's not moving away from town. He's taking a job as personnel co-ordinator for Bomex."

Ah. Jan remembered the ladies in red jackets in the hotel. Had she missed a hint, then, a chance, or had she escaped?

"Bomex may take over Cartwright's. That was why Mr Livermore tried to do the superman bit over Ellis and Miss Baldwin. He wanted to impress. But I'm afraid he'll be out under the New Order; they have their own stock of the older generation."

Automatically Jan asked:

"Will you take David's job?"

"I think they'll appoint someone over my head. A man. I don't know if I'll fight it. I'm not all that competitive."

She looked carefully at Jan.

"But if we go into the Bomex Group, there will be a lot of chances for someone young and with drive."

Oh ah. I'd look great in a red jacket. In a pig's ear.

"Why didn't he tell me?" Was she asking Margaret Hardwick or talking to herself? Margaret Hardwick waited a moment before replying.

"I expect he chickened out, like I did. It's not easy when you know people will be hurt."

So, he wanted not to hurt her feelings.

"I expect we shall see him now and then. He'll probably buy a house here or nearby, and have his family with him."

Family? Oh yes, she knew where he would buy a house.

"So he's not moved then?"

Margaret Hardwick seemed puzzled.

"I don't think so. Not yet."

Jan stood on the pavement as Margaret Hardwick drove away. She felt suddenly light-headed. Instead of going indoors, she set off at a run away from the street. As she hurried, the thoughts arranged themselves, like someone casually dealing cards. If David was not in Cartwright's any more, then no one would know about his private life. How would they know if she saw him now and then – just for this while – before his family were there? She could arrange herself a little holiday from life, a little box of chocolates, something to chew to keep the taste in the mouth, and no one else would know. And would he play? Why wouldn't he? He'd managed all this while and enjoyed it. "You seduced me," he said. Well, she had, hadn't she, and she'd enjoyed it as well. So why all the misery? Who's to know? Who's to care? Why not?

Outside his flat she scribbled a note. "Still alive and well, and . . . J", pushed it under the door and ran home.

She stayed home in the cold evenings, sat with her books, watched the box and played endless losing games with her quick-witted little brother. She had polite cups of tea with Dad, and Sandra too. And did all this with a fraction of her mind, while all the rest connected to her ear and that turned like a crouching animal's to the faint sound, the ting that signalled the ringing of the phone. Then she would move with silent speed and snatch it from the hook, hold it up and shout to the stairs, "For you, Dad."

Three nights of this were all that she could stand. Now she began first furtively, then brazenly, to ring his number, after breakfast, once or twice during the day, when Margaret Hardwick was out of the room and at intervals through the evening. There was no answer, ever, and soon all feeling and interest in the feeling ebbed away leaving her mind dry and bare.

Depression made her listless and she worked by willpower only, willpower fuelled by pride. Outside, the wind, the driving rain, the leaves lying in sodden heaps, the dank days and dark evenings closed in and contained her mood.

Then something happened, a small thing. She set out in mid-evening and passed down his street. The window blankly caught the lamplight, gleamed and signalled her to move on. She wandered to the pub and pushed through the doors. The bar was almost empty and she turned to go out

"Hey, Jan."

Peter Carey sat alone at a table just inside the door, half-empty glass in front of him. He rose and grinned.

"Tonic?"

She made a face. She ought to go. But she stayed. She sat down, unbuttoned her coat and stayed. Were they both waiting, filling in time?"

"Just finished a shift," he explained. "Always a bit wound up after a broadcast. Have to get down a gear before I go home."

"Still living . . .?"

He grinned: "Right. Our mum can be a pain but it is the most comfortable pad I know. I ought to move out. It can be inconvenient. But she'd rather I stayed. And Dad's away a lot. It seems only fair."

He hesitated, then, "Jan. I'm sorry about that other time you were in here. It was not my idea to land on you and ask about Cartwright's."

Oh, she knew that, it wasn't him. It was the road manager, wasn't it?

"Forget it," she said. "How's the job?"

"Great. Makes me wonder if I really want to go to college after all. You know half of us go on studying because we're expected to. Supposed to be good for you, makes you grow, like cod-liver oil."

She grinned, felt relaxed for the first time in – years. This was P. Carey at his best, chatty, thoughtful, charming. It was, she recalled, six months since they had talked like this.

"It's been a long time," he said.

"Right."

Pause.

"I never had a bust-up like that before with anyone," he said.

She couldn't say that, could she?

"I've always taken it easy, moved on before it got heavy – my motto."

"Slipped up there, Carey."

Only his sudden glance told her that she had spoken aloud. He grinned: "That's better."

"What d'you mean – better?"

"Well, to be honest, Whitfield, when you came through that door you looked like death warmed up."

"Ta very much. Nicely turned compliment."

"I saw you come in a couple of times before. I was over the other side. You didn't see me. You were looking for somebody else."

Oh yes.

His voice lowered, became gentler.

"Giving you a hard time?"

She began to shake her head, then – what the hell – she nodded.

"Bloke at work?"

Another nod.

"Sod."

She couldn't nod to that – except in her mind.

"Want to talk about it?"

"Nope."

She got up.

"Thanks, Pete. That's a kind thought, but I'm not issuing any statements at the moment."

"OK." He raised his glass as she turned in the doorway.

"Give us a bell, if . . ."

She nodded.

If.

31

Work and other people. The cure?

Jan looked at the dirty dishes on the draining board – last night and breakfast. Dad was out, taking Kevin and the two herberts next door on a trip to Manchester. Then there was the cleaning.

She pulled the apron off its hook, started to tie it on, then flung it down, marched into the hall, snatched her coat and went out. The cold struck her in the face and made her catch her breath. But that was just for an instant. The sky was deep blue and the sun was lurking somewhere beyond the rooftops. She caught up with it in the park where it hung low and red, casting long shadows across the white grass. In the still frosted air the last leaves fell like rain and lay in fresh pools of colour round each tree, maroon round the copper beech, orange for the mountain ash, light gold for the silver birch.

She breathed out, childishly pleased with the white puff of vapour from her lips. She walked faster, striding out until she reached the river and turned along the towpath. As she came by the allotments she stopped in surprise. The tiny figure of her neighbour was there, bending and standing up, resting a hand on hip, then bending again. Around her the earth, newly dug, showed black brown. The old girl had cleared half the plot. Weeds and old vegetables were piled up in a neat heap.

She turned as Jan came up.

"Hello, love. You caught me unawares. I was just planting."

"What, in December?"

"Oh ah, broad beans. There's a lot grows in winter,

more than you'd think. If you plant 'em now, it keeps off the black fly – they reckon. Ooh," she rubbed her hip again.

Jan took the bean packet and dibbing stick and began to put the seeds into the soil along the line of string.

"That's it when you've done that," the old woman was cleaning spade and fork. "I've got business back home." Jan finished the row and looked at Mrs Elsom. The dour resignation of the day of the funeral was gone. The voice was light, even perky.

She took the tools and they walked back together.

"What are you up to then, Mrs . . .?"

"Oh, call me Edie, love."

They turned into the street.

"I'm having the place done up."

"Get away."

"I am an' all. You know what they say. Widowers re-marry, widows redecorate."

She pushed open the front door.

"Come in and have a cup of coffee. It's all in a mess."

"So's mine."

Gossiping like an old hen.

They stood in the kitchen, table and cooker covered in sheets, walls half-stripped. Mrs Elsom began to put the kettle on. Jan looked round.

"Are you doing it yourself – Edie?"

"Get off with your bother. I've got a bloke coming in to do the papering. But I'll save a bit by stripping it myself."

She swung the steaming kettle and pushed cups onto a corner of the table. They sat down and grinned at one another.

"You know, Jan, our Joe was one of the best but he was a stick-in-the-mud. 'What's wrong with the wallpaper?' he'd say. And it'd been up for twenty years. I put up with it for his sake. Didn't want to upset him. But now I'm sure he wouldn't mind, aren't you?"

They finished the coffee in silence, then Mrs Elsom looked shyly at Jan.

"I'll show you something else."

Jan followed her up the stairs. It was the same as her own home, only left-handed. But no, not quite. This was one of the houses with an attic bedroom. Mrs Elsom led the way in.

It was low and large. A white wood wall hid the tanks and cistern. A single bed, iron bedstead covered by an embroidered quilt, a white dressing table with tiny pots and mats, a wardrobe and chest of drawers. By it stood a tennis racket in an old canvas case. On top were school books and a photograph, the same picture as downstairs, the serious face looked out, shy and bold at the same time. The room was spotless, not a speck of dust.

"Our Brenda's."

"But it's . . ." began Jan

"I know, love. You wouldn't believe. It's been like this for over forty years. Joe wanted it kept. He often used to come and sit here. Look, you can see over to Borley Top from the window. He'd sit and look out, and think."

Jan sat on the broad, low window ledge. Way across the rooftops, beyond chimneys and tower blocks, was a clear space where the moors rose distant and purple in the winter sunshine. And above them the bare crown of Borley Top. The old girl was talking again. Jan half heard, then remembered the words later.

"You can understand it in a way. You see, I didn't want her to go. I was glad I had a girl. I thought, if I had a boy, they'd take him, and send him off when the war came. But she wanted to join up. She was barely older than you. She had a scholarship. She'd not long left school. But she wanted to go. She volunteered. I said I didn't want her to.

But Joe said, let her go. She'll be all right. Between the two of them, she got her way."

"Anyway in the end she was on one of the anti-aircraft guns. They had girls on them, you know. She'd been there for a year and then there was a big raid and they were hit with incendiary bombs. There was a fire. She pulled her mate out, then she went back because she thought there was somebody else. Then some of the shells went up."

There was a long pause.

"She got a medal. Well, we got it. I should have put my foot down, I should have been selfish. I shouldn't have let her go. Mothers always lose out."

Another pause.

"Come on down, love. I'm going to clear it all out. There's dresses in there, even her gymslip. The lot's going. I don't know if I need redecorate, but I'll clear out, just keep the picture."

She made a swinging movement with her hand.

"What d'you reckon?"

"It's a lovely room. You could let it out, I suppose."

Edie led the way downstairs, calling back over her shoulder.

"Not likely. I'm not having a stranger up there."

They paused by the front door.

"But if you ever want a little place to be by yourself in, you know, when things get too much, you're welcome."

"Me?"

"Yes, love. I notice things."

She leaned up and gave Jan a quick peck on the cheek.

"Come in and give us a hand sometime, any road."

On impulse Jan turned back, rolled up her sleeves and helped strip the kitchen. It was satisfying to pull at the loose edges and feel the long sheets of paper peel back leaving the plaster bare and grey beneath. They worked into the afternoon, until Jan realised she must go. Then they sat down together and ate in comfortable silence.

Back in her own home, Jan began to do the chores she had abandoned in the morning. She worked reluctantly and with increasing irritability as she moved from kitchen to front room, then upstairs to the bedrooms. She must be more tired than she realised. It had been a wearing week.

In Dad's room, she scooped up papers onto bed and desk and began to vacuum the floor. The machine swung to and fro, then struck the wardrobe. One door flew open and Jan stared, disbelievingly. She snapped on the light. It was dark outside now. The wardrobe was half empty. The rail had been cleared. The rest of Mum's clothes had gone.

As she made tea downstairs, she heard the car draw up in the street. The front door burst open and Kevin tumbled in, clutching boxes and carrier bags. Dad called from the doorway.

"Jan, can you put the lad to bed, please? And take that gear off him. He's not having it till Christmas. I'll be back later."

On Sunday morning, Jan tapped lightly on Dad's door. Kevin was downstairs. She went in. Dad looked up in surprise from his desk.

"What's up?"

"What have you done with . . .?" she did not finish the sentence but gestured to the wardrobe door.

"Oh, the dresses?" He looked away out of the window. "I let Sandra have them. No point leaving them there."

"You what?"

Her voice rose. He looked alarmed. Then he spoke in a low voice.

"What are you on about? I let you have some of them. But you're not wearing them any more."

"Well, I still don't think you ought to hand them out like that."

163

"So, it's all right to give them to you, when you don't wear them, and not all right to give them to Sandra . . .?"

"There's a difference . . ."

"What difference?"

"They're Mum's dresses. She'd have let me have some of them. There's no way she'd have let Sandra have them."

He flushed: "I don't care for the way you talk lately. You act a lot too grown up. You're only seventeen, actually."

"I know, you told me before."

She said no more but walked out of the room and back to her own. She sat by the window, looking at the houses opposite.

32

Next Sunday, in the grey winter afternoon, Jan climbed the streets to Margaret Hardwick's house.

"You need cheering up," the older woman had said. "Come and have tea and we'll chat about – anything you like."

The house was double-fronted, of grey-brown local stone and stood back from the road with a dark green apron of lawn and shrubs spread out in front of it. Margaret Hardwick was waiting by the open front door. She wore a blouse embroidered with a pattern of reds, greens and browns. She smiled.

"I can see all the way down the hill. I spotted you at the end of the road. Let's do the inspection bit first and then we can sit down in peace and quiet."

She led the way from one high-ceilinged, low-silled room to another.

"It's nearly dusk now, you can't see so far. But come up again when the light days come back. This is why I bought it. I reckon on a clear day I can see Derbyshire from this window, Yorkshire from this, Lancashire from the bathroom, if I stand on a chair, and down into Cheshire from the kitchen."

She looked at Jan, a little embarrassed.

"It's too big, isn't it? The mortgage itself takes half my pay. I rattle in it. But it's my fortress. Come on, let's eat."

Tea was laid in a room lit only by lamps on small tables. Curtains were half drawn, leaving a view of the western sky streaked with red that faded as they talked, while the pools of light thrown on the floor grew stronger. Their faces were in shadow and that made it easier for Jan to talk. She was hungry, too; sandwiches, salad, cakes went so quickly that she apologised.

"Go on," urged Margaret Hardwick. "Appetite's always bigger when someone else makes the meal. I eat very little on my own, but I like company. I like sharing a meal. I have too many alone."

I'd love to have meals on my own, thought Jan. But she said nothing. Her host was talking again.

"Jan, let's have a girl to girl talk. We're out of the office. Neither of us will breathe a word. And call me Margaret, please. You've had a hard knock over David. I watched it, saw it coming. I should have spoken. I didn't. When you live in a man's world, as I do, you pick up some of their habits. It's called solidarity."

Jan looked down and waited in silence. Outside it was now completely dark.

"David's a special sort of man. He's ambitious, he's energetic. He's very masculine in some ways."

You're telling me, thought Jan wryly.

"But he's kind and gentle. He's not domineering with women colleagues. He's polite. Doesn't interrupt, doesn't make excuses to put his hand round your shoulder – or anywhere else for that matter. He's a very dangerous type."

Margaret laughed quietly. "With women, he'll wait and see what they will do. Personally, I mean. It's as though he'd be pleased if you fell for him, but didn't want any blame for what happens."

Her voice became lower. "I did not come to the office until after your mother left. I can only guess about how he behaved towards her. But I'm sure he was helpful and kind. And sometimes, I think, she may have found herself being drawn into a relationship she couldn't control."

"What do you mean?" Jan's voice was sharp.

"Oh, I don't think anything happened – like that. But a

woman will know if something is going to. She knows that sometimes one move from her will make everything change. At that moment, you can either put up the stop sign, or you can . . ."

"Just clear off," whispered Jan.

Margaret did not seem to hear her. "You took him by surprise, I think. You didn't wait to see what would happen. You moved. People don't find it easy to cope with a girl like you, Jan. You are incredibly impulsive."

Jan heard David's voice: "You seduced me."

Margaret was on her feet collecting the tea things together.

"Let me help," said Jan.

They went together into the kitchen. It was cool and bright and the equipment gleamed. It was the kind of kitchen Jan thought about at home. She picked up the tea towel and looked around as Margaret began to pass cups and saucers saying: "I don't own a machine, not enough use for it."

Jan was not listening. She had spotted a poster on the wall – an artist's work: a great circular table, smooth doll-like children bending over plates and at the centre, a figure serving from a great dish.

"It's ceramic, pottery," said Margaret. "By a Hungarian, she's called Margaret, too, Margaret Kovacs. It's called *The Big Family*."

She blushed: "I've always wanted a family, but I've never met someone I could – commit myself to. I always held back. Perhaps it's too late now."

They had drifted back into the other room. Margaret switched on the overhead lamp.

"I'll show you some more of the pictures. I've got postcard reproductions."

She began to search through a drawer in the corner and then came back to place a bundle of cards in Jan's hands and sat down again next to her. Jan turned the cards without seeing, then:

"Can I ask you about something, Margaret?"

"Of course."

Slowly and with much hesitation, then in a rush, Jan told about things at home, about Dad and Kevin, about housework, about money, even about Mum's dresses, and of course, about Sandra. The words poured out as she turned the postcards in her hands.

Margaret put an arm round Jan's shoulder.

"I don't know what to say, Jan love. Your mother's gone. It does seem, after what is it, eight, nine months, she isn't coming back. For your father that changes things." She paused. "You know, I met him in the summer, at one of the management course get-togethers, when firms go head-hunting. He's a man with drive. He's quiet, but single-minded. He will go places, don't worry. He won't wait around to see what happens."

She laid a hand on Jan's wrist, stopping the slightly feverish flipping of the postcards.

"Didn't it occur to you that your father might want to start again – with someone else? Very soon your mother will have been away for a whole year. That changes the situation about divorce. Things can't stand still. Since she isn't here any more, and . . ."

Jan suddenly held up a card. The sculptured figures were rough, reddish-brown. A young women embraced an older one. The older face looked out around the younger shoulders, pleadingly. She turned the card. The caption read:

"Who is now the mother, who the daughter?"

She looked at Margaret, whose face was quite close.

"Would you mind if I kept this one?" she said.

33

As Christmas drew nearer, Jan's life entered a brief period of calm. The pace eased off at Cartwright's, the atmosphere relaxed. David Thompson's office stayed empty. No one was appointed to his job and Margaret Hardwick took over his work. She did not ask Jan to stay late, and Jan wondered to herself now and then how much of the pressure had been raised by David's personality, though for all she knew, Margaret Hardwick was simply packing away the extra problems and working over them beneath the lamplight while the winter dark gathered around her comfortable fortress up there on the hill.

After their talk over the tea cups, their conversation was only of work, and everyday things, as if neither of them wanted to probe deeper into the life of the other. Jan kept to herself all the thoughts stirred by the talk just as she kept the postcard picture of the mother and daughter in her bag, to look at when she was quiet and on her own.

When she had asked for it that day, Margaret had looked at her strangely but handed it to her. Jan studied the figures, the lowered, sad face of the older woman, the strong, turned shoulders of the younger and then the thought struck her:

"Hey, you said it was a statue, didn't you?"

"Well, a sculpture."

"Yes, well, I mean this picture only shows one side. On the other side there'll be the face of the young woman, won't there?"

"I suppose so," Margaret hadn't seemed interested.

"You saw it in the exhibition, didn't you? I mean, where

169

you got the poster and the cards. Can't you remember how it looked from the other side?"

Margaret smiled and shook her head.

"Sorry, Jan, but honestly I can't. Everybody who goes round an exhibition remembers different things. I just bought all the postcards they had. I'm afraid I didn't pay attention to that one. Sure you still want the card?"

"Oh yes."

Oh yes. The card had become something of a charm to her. She could take it out when she was up in her room and look at it. And a strange sad peace came stealing into her mind and she could feel her tangled thoughts unwind and rearrange themselves. But what they told her was not certain – yet. What was certain was that when she looked at the card, she saw, in her mind's eye, the attic room next door, and the view of Borley Top from the window.

She began to prepare for Christmas, half from memory of how they used to do it, half making it up as she went along. She bought presents – Dad, Kev, Gran, Grandad, for people at work – something special for Penny.

She chose decorations. She thought that maybe each room could be different this time. She checked the money carefully, and planned the extra food, and thought to herself she'd buy nuts ready shelled. Blow Kev, he didn't clear up afterwards, or he always seemed to wriggle out of it. Then she felt guilty and bought half shelled, half unshelled.

Meals: Christmas Day was taken care of. It would be Christmas dinner and tea at Warby, and back home so stuffed your eyes popped out. Gran and Grandad would put on an extra show this Christmas. It was the first like this, wasn't it?

But Boxing Day – what about Boxing Day? They'd be on their own. Then she thought, why not invite Edie? That would make four. She put the problem to Harry. His red face turned serious and he put the huge head on one side: "Pork joint, leg of lamb. Everybody's up to here with bird on Boxing Day, dear. That's it – four, you said. I'll keep you a pork joint and you can . . ." he began to go over the cooking details and the women in the shop chuckled behind Jan's back. But it put her in a good mood. On the way home another thought struck her. And after tea that night, when little brother was out of the way she said:

"Dad, can we discuss Christmas arrangements?"

"Eh?" he looked surprised. "Warby, like always." He stressed the "always".

"No, I mean general arrangements, not just Christmas Day."

"Oh," he shrugged. He was already on his feet. "Look Jan, I've got a lot to do. I'll think about it and let you know. I'll work something out. OK?"

Well no, it wasn't actually, but . . .

"Dad," she burst out as he reached the door, "there is one thing. I'd like to invite someone for tea, Sunday afternoon before Christmas – someone from work."

"Oh, ah?"

"Yes, it's Margaret Hardwick – who I work for. She says she's met you."

He stood half out of the door way, face blank.

"Oh, OK, but do you mind if I don't join you, like?"

"Oh Dad, you can't do that. Look. Can you not be there just for the eating bit?"

"Oh, all right. I'll slip off afterwards. OK?"

OK.

But as it turned out, everything went well. Margaret Hardwick was actually pleased to be invited; she reddened slightly when Jan asked her. She drove up dead on four o'clock with a massive box of chocolates and flowers.

Dad, Jan noticed, was reserved and almost shy, though when the conversation turned on work, on changes in management, then he took charge and was forceful and direct. He stayed longer after the meal than Jan had expected before excusing himself and going to his room.

Kevin was taken by the visitor. She proved to be an enthusiast for anything from jigsaws to Trivial Pursuit and Jan was a spectator while the two of them contested, wrangled and joked. That, thought Jan, is what you do when you live on your own, you revert, you play games again. She wished she was not so bored by these things which so gripped her young brother. But watching them made her feel about a hundred.

"I have to go."

Margaret was on her feet. Kevin protested.

"Oh, come and see me and have tea in the New Year, lad," she grinned at him. "Your dad, or Jan can bring you. They don't have to stay. I'm bound to get a new game for Christmas. If someone doesn't buy me one, I'll buy one myself."

"Great." Kev leapt for the front door and held it open. There was a gent inside the lad, struggling to get out.

On the pavement outside, he capered and waved. Jan stood, arms folded. Dad had said goodbye briefly and returned to his room. But there was someone else at the farewell too.

As the car drove off and Kev barged back into the house, she saw out of the corner of her eye the quick flick of the curtain falling on the window of Sandra's front room.

34

They were sitting round the dinner table the following Saturday when Dad said casually:

"Right, well, I think I've sorted Christmas out."

Oh.

"Boxing Day's the problem. We can't sit here, just the three of us, so I thought we'd do a combined meal."

Combined?

He saw she was baffled.

"Yes. It's daft if Sandra and her boys sit next door eating one lot of grub while we sit here and eat ours. So, if we invite them in, it'll make a bit of a party of it."

Jan's voice was small. "I've only ordered a pork joint."

"Well, you can change that, can't you? Any road, Sandra'll have something, chicken or whatever."

"And who's going to do it all?"

He stared at her, was about to speak sharply, when he remembered Kevin was there across the table, excited, ears twitching.

"Oh, I'm sure Sandra will help. I mean it'd be a way of saying thanks for all the help she's given us."

Oh, I thought that had been taken care of. For a sickening moment Jan believed she had actually spoken the words. But no, her tight-pressed lips had trapped them.

"And there's maybe a Christmas show for the day after."

"Yeah – *Space Fantasy* at the Troc," Kev was putting in his twopennorth now.

Jan got up and began clearing the dishes.

"I need to think about it. I had thought of asking you,"

she somehow underlined the word "asking", "if we could invite Mrs Elsom in on Boxing Day. She's really on her own."

"Good lord, why not? Why didn't you say? She can come as well." Dad spoke very quickly. Jan put the dishes on the draining board and left the room. She took her coat from the hall and went out, walking rapidly down the road, through the brightly lit shopping centre in the chill afternoon light and then back through the side streets, her feet pounding the pavements to the rhythm of her thoughts.

When she got back the dishes had been washed, the cloth shaken and folded. The sight of it seemed to sharpen her inner feelings, half anger half nausea.

The television was on in the front room. Were they both in there? She climbed the stairs. A light showed under Dad's door. She tiptoed on past to her own room. She was ready to have this out, but not yet. There was no place in this house for a really good row. If they had a place like Margaret's they could go into one of those high-ceilinged rooms and shout and march about and turn on one another.

But it wasn't going to be like that, she knew. Beneath all the anger and frustration, all the childish heat, there was a cool tiredness, like an older person, waiting to take over, if she could just hold on.

A knock on her door froze her thoughts. Dad was in the doorway. Awkwardly she got up. They both stood facing each other, then he moved across and pulled on the curtains, closing them more tightly. Now they were walled in and there was no avoiding this any more. To her relief she felt the heat inside begin to die down. He spoke quietly, but that seemed to sharpen what he said:

"Jan, just what are you after?"

"I don't know what you mean."

"I mean down there," he pointed as if to pin down the

conversation in the kitchen. "What's your real objection to my plans for Christmas?"

"I didn't say." She began to protest. She knew it was silly but couldn't help it.

"I know you didn't. You looked. You forget I've known you a long time. I know what looks mean."

She spoke, at last, calmly, her words ordering themselves as she talked:

"For one I objected to just being told. I know, when we were kids, you used to tell us what'd happen at Christmas. But that was then. Now I'm supposed to be running things – I mean running the house – yes, and paying for it."

"Oh yes. But you'd invited the old girl next door, hadn't you? You'd made your plans."

"I never . . ." She controlled herself. "As it happens, I haven't. I was going to ask you before I spoke to her."

His gaze lowered. She followed up.

"But you'd already asked Sandra, hadn't you?"

Now he was going to protest but she gave no room.

"It was Sandra's idea, wasn't it? You discuss a lot of domestic things with her, don't you?"

His lips tightened. She rushed on.

"When are we going to take her with us to Warby, eh?"

"You have no right," his voice rose, then fell, "no right to say things like that. Absolutely no right."

"I'm sorry," the two words were pushed out between her teeth. He was calmer, so was she now the words had been spoken. They both knew what it was all about. It was not about Christmas. It was about the future. The time of truce was over, the time of pretending nothing had happened was over. The battle was on about how it was to be.

"Dad, I don't want to quarrel with you about Sandra. If you want to invite her round here, with those boys of hers, that's up to you. It is your house. It is just this. If that is how it is going to be, I shall move out. I don't want to get in your way, but Sandra and I don't mix."

"Where to?"

"Not far. Mrs Elsom's got a room I can have. It's a nice room. I'll move out as soon as I've finished getting things in for Christmas. I'm sure you'll be able to manage between . . ."

He burst through her words.

"You can't move out. You're not eighteen. You're still my responsibility."

A silence fell while they both considered what he had said. But she discovered that somewhere deep in her own mind, she had thought about all this.

"OK. You make me stay here. You've told me often enough, I'm only seventeen. I'm not grown up yet. So we'll do it that way. I'll do what you tell me, and that's that. But as far as running things goes, that's finished. I'll pay my keep. I'll do my share. But I'll be a kid, like I used to be. I'll grumble, I'll be stroppy, I'll wriggle out of things, a bit like Kev. I expect I'll forget things. I'll be late and oversleep. I could do with a rest from pretending to be an adult. It's no big deal from what I can see."

She stopped the line of thought before it went too far.

"Look, Dad. I'll stay if you make me. But I'd rather go. I think it's fairer to Kev and you if I did. I'm the odd one out."

"That's not true. We both need you. And Kev, have you thought about Kev? He's supposed to have a family. He's lost his mother. Is he going to lose his sister?"

"Yes, his big sister. She looks after him and he cheeks her, and ignores what she says, then plays up to her when he's alone with her. And, when Sandra's in here, he's downright rude to me. I love him I suppose, but just lately I've begun to dislike him. I have no control over what he does or you do. I'm a dogsbody. A skivvy. I've taken Mum's place, like Gran said I should, but without the

176

respect. You still want to order me about and tell me how old I'm not. Yes, that's why Boxing Day was the last straw. It's a family day and if Mum were here now, there is no way Sandra would come over the front doorstep."

"So, that's what it's about after all," he said, "despite all the discussions we had, despite the fact that you seemed to agree when we talked it over? Despite all the time that's gone. Despite the fact that she went off and left us, yes you as well, despite all that, all you can say is I want my mum back."

She considered the words as if there was no edge to them.

"Yes," she said slowly, "I do want her back. Oh, I do. But for a different reason than when we talked about it in the summer. Not just to fill a gap in my life, not just like an extra blanket on the bed when it's cold at night. I want to know how she is."

Her voice rose, then dropped again, becoming softer.

"I want to know how she is. I want to know if she's happy. I want to know if she's alive or dead."

He shook his head as if to fend off the words.

"She's not coming back, you know that."

"Well, if she won't come back, I'll go and find her. I'll look and search until I find her. Dad," she blinked, "I'm moving out. Don't stop me, please."

He breathed deeply. His face was calmer now.

"I won't stop you. Do what you like."

He looked suddenly worried.

"You'll come to Warby, won't you?"

She almost laughed.

"'Course I'm coming to Warby."

"And you'll say nowt to them?"

She nodded. "Not a word."

35

Dad surprised Jan by stepping forward, kissing her, and saying, "Goodnight, Jan," and going out, almost as if he were relieved at the way things had turned out.

There was nothing new or surprising in what they'd said. They were just, she thought as she moved about the room tidying things, carrying on the big sort out they'd begun months ago, at the start of the summer holiday. Then he had silenced her – taking the fourth chair out from under the kitchen table.

Now it was back there. He was free again and so was she, free to think about Mum as she liked, or not to think about her, free to look for her, or leave her wandering through the world. She took out the postcard from her bag and looked at it for a while before she made ready for bed. That night she slept like a child and if she had dreams she forgot them when she awoke.

Next day she packed things in her suitcase. There wasn't really very much. She had travelled light so far. Perhaps now she had a real room of her own she'd gather knick-knacks and ugly woolly animals and posters for the wall, and buy books to read just for fun, and get a writing case and write letters to people:

"I'm sitting in my room from where I can see the moors and Borley Top. Do you remember how we used to go walking up there? Dad and Kev used to lag behind didn't they . . .?"

She snapped the case shut. That'd do for a start. She could carry dresses and that separately. It wasn't the end of the earth – just next door. Still, it was a long way.

"You're kidding." Kev's eyes had a funny look.

"I'm not."

"Where are you going?"

He was anxious. She was suddenly ashamed.

"Next door."

"What?"

"No, dimmo." Not that next door. She jerked her head to the right, away, away from Sandra's.

"Oh." He made it a long word.

"You can come and see me if you like – if you're very good." She ruffled his hair. "Get Dad to bring you in the car."

Then he remembered something. His eyes narrowed,

"Can I still go for tea – to Auntie Margaret's?"

Auntie?

"You wally. 'Course you can. She invited you. She keeps her promises. But for crying out loud, don't call her Auntie, or she'll have your guts for garters."

Now he was relieved.

On her way home from work, she called in at Harry's and asked him to make the Boxing Day order a small bird after all. She'd make a second Christmas Day with Edie. With a bottle of wine. They'd get tiddly and sing silly songs.

And they did.

Christmas came and went before she knew. Her time away from work was taken up with shopping and stripping wallpaper. Some nights she stayed up working on the house until the small hours and still got up chirpy to go to work. Margaret Hardwick looked at her now and then but made no comment. Their friendship was a friendly, easy one. To Jan she seemed like an elder sister she had never had, someone she knew she could talk to if she needed. And because she was sure of this and treasured it, she trod carefully in the office, remembering Margaret Hardwick was boss. Their friendship was a thing apart and she liked to think Margaret valued it as she did.

Christmas Day went as planned. As they drove to Warby, across the moors white with frost, she sensed Dad was anxious, looking at her now and then. But not a word was said about what had passed between them. Even little Big Mouth did his bit and kept the secret between the three of them. For him it was part of a game and she suspected he was hoping that it might turn out to be permanent and he could take over her room.

Gran was pleased with them all. Her Geoff was doing well. Grandad proposed a toast to Dad's success next year when he would surely get the post he deserved.

"But don't get too posh, our Geoff."

"Give over, our Dad."

Then Grandad went on to toast our Jan who'd make a big career for herself. Gran kept her peace. And Dad, as if to reassure everyone, drank down his beer and said:

"Well, if Bomex take over Cartwright's, we may be working for the same outfit."

"And Auntie Margaret as well," said Kev.

Dad frowned.

"Who?" demanded Grandad.

"Just someone at work," said Jan hastily.

"Right, let's be having you then," said Grandad. "In next door and see what we've got under the Christmas tree."

As they drove home, Dad turned to Jan and said: "Perhaps you'd like to start driving lessons again in the New Year?"

She smiled to herself.

"I'll think about it," she said.

36

Boxing Day and the two days after were lazy days. Jan luxuriated in long lie-ins. She had moved bed and chest of drawers around so that she could lie and look out of the window at the distant moors. And the sun, at its rising and its setting, looking sideways into her hideout, made small golden patches on the wall where it met the ceiling.

There'd be a little knock on the door.

"Cup of tea, Jan?"

And she'd answer lazily.

"Down in a bit, Edie."

Between them they dressed the half-decorated house with bits of holly and paper lanterns.

"Don't overdo it, Jan love," murmured Mrs Elsom. "Too much of a good thing."

Jan laughed and hugged her.

New Year's Eve was the annual party at Cartwright's. Jan hesitated about going, but was urged on.

"Get away with you, Jan. You've been stuck in the house, working like a Trojan for days. You get out and have a good time. You've got your key. Just don't fall over when you come upstairs, that's all."

That evening she found herself ready to go out far too early. For some reason she was impatient like a little girl before a party. She looked at her watch – six thirty. Good grief, another couple of hours. She wasn't going to stand around in a half-empty canteen at work while the band (Cartwright's were a little old-fashioned in this) warmed up and people looked one another over.

On impulse she picked up the directory and looked up Peak Radio. She dialled the number. It rang, and rang.

Then a slightly slurred man's voice answered.

"Peak-a-Radio. Can I – a – help you?"

"Can I speak to Peter Carey, please?"

"Well you can, love, if you struggle round to the Golden Lion and rescue him from the claws of half the women in the firm. They're having a do."

"Eh. Have they left you behind?"

"In the ashes, dear." He paused. "Want to join me?"

"That is kind of you. But I'm off to the ball."

"Just my luck. Happy New Year."

"Same to you."

She found Pete in the bar. It was jammed and lively with shouting and singing.

Mr Carey was in high spirits with a paper hat on the side of his dark curly head. He had a girl on each arm and they were dancing, or rather swaying to and fro in the crush.

"Hey, Jan! Happy New Year."

He leaned forward like a trapeze artist, supported by his partners and kissed her. The girls tried to pull him back towards them, but he skilfully slid out of their grasp and laid his hands on Jan's shoulders. A wave of music blasted over the shouting and singing and they were dancing, Pete singing some unofficial lines to the melody. They bumped against each other and others around them. Someone pushed past her throwing her closer. She looked up and he kissed her, a longer one. She suddenly felt light-headed.

She shouted in his ear.

"If only you were sober."

"If only you were stoned," he answered.

"Where's Sharon?" she asked mischievously.

He rolled his eyes.

"I decided we needed a rest."

"What did she say?"

He didn't answer. His hands moved in to Jan's neck and began to caress the skin beneath her hair. Ah, Mr Carey was having a rest all right, or perhaps a holiday from Sharon. But she doubted Sharon realised that yet. Oh no, Jan, she thought. Not like that again, not even on the rebound from you know who.

"Got to go, Pete."

"Why? Where? How? With whom? For what reason?"

"You have your office party, I have mine."

He bent his face to hers. She kissed him and lifted his hands from her shoulder. He made a face.

"See you around, Carey."

"Life's before us, Whitfield."

She struggled away to the door, but allowed herself one quick look back. He was dancing again, but with a different girl. He didn't look up.

Cartwright's' New Year do was well under way when she got to the works. The music was straight down the middle, classic pop numbers and Palm Court scored for brass. Round the floor people danced their own dances, their own styles. Older women sat around at crowded tables, gossiping and drinking. Groups of white collar men clustered round the management end, talking shop. Jan moved around, talked to people, greeted Margaret and sat down to have a sandwich and a drink with her.

"Where's Penny?" she asked

Margaret smiled

"Very busy liaising with the Accounts Department."

She nodded to their right. Jan spotted Penny, splendidly untidy in a long blue gown, with a sash already unwinding, hair in her eyes, dancing with a thin young man with glasses. The contrast in their heights ought to have been comic, but it wasn't. Jan felt suddenly relieved, though why she couldn't think. Then she remembered someone else.

She left Margaret and began to circle the room. She danced with solemn, correct, Rodney Mulcaster from Accounts.

"Will you stay with us in the New Year, Janice, or move on to higher things?"

"Oh, I'm in no hurry to move."

"Good, we need young people like you."

"Thank you."

Out of the corner of her eye, she saw Vikki Cooper dancing determinedly with the managing director. She left Mulcaster and moved on, exchanged grins with Penny, skilfully avoided being massaged round the hall by Charlie Sims from Sales and found herself back near Margaret Hardwick's table again. So far she had not seen Tina.

She stopped by a table full of women from Production. They stopped their chat and laughter for a moment.

"Tina? Haven't seen her. As a matter of fact she hasn't been in since the break, has she? Had a lot of time off lately."

"Thanks. I'll look around."

It was nine o'clock. Jan found her coat and stepped out of the dining hall, leaving the warmth and noise for the still, cold air. She braced herself, hugged the coat round her and set out walking briskly. The sky was full of stars, brilliant and distant, and over to the south there was the edge of a rising moon.

Ten minutes brought her to Tina's house. The front room window curtains were closed. But the room was lit. Someone was in watching the box. She knocked and waited. There was no bell. No answer. She thumped on the door and waited. No sign. She turned to go, then thought, no, be damned. She rapped on the window pane sharply with her knuckles. The curtain was pulled on one side and Tina's face looked out, alarmed, angry, then the curtain dropped. A moment later the front door half opened. Tina was in a dressing gown, face pale.

"Yes?" the one word was neither welcoming nor hostile.

"I came to see how you were."

"You can see."

"Tina," Jan was calm. "Let's come in. You'll catch your death and so will I."

Tina moved back and the two of them went into the front room. It's smaller than ours, thought Jan. A half-finished meal and a glass of lager stood on a kitchen stool.

"You weren't at the do. I came to see."

Tina switched off the television, turned to look at Jan. Her voice was flat but it seemed near to breaking.

"No, I am not at the bloody do. I am stuck here."

"Couldn't you get someone to look after these kids? I mean neighbours."

"Neighbours? You must be joking."

Tina sat down suddenly on the settee. The movement knocked the stool, the meal scattered, the lager poured foaming into the carpet. Jan bent to pick things up, then heard the awful grating sound of Tina's crying. She heaved herself up, sat down beside Tina and pulled her head onto her shoulder.

"Tina, love, what is it?"

"Ever since he got the push, he's been worse. He's drinking his compo money, when he isn't betting. He's off for days at a time. He tried to bring his women round here, but I put my foot down. I'll walk out I said. He believed me, thank Christ, though I couldn't have. I won't let anything happen to the twins and our Gary.

"He's rowed with everyone on the street. Nobody wants to know. And if they do, who wants to baby-sit here, when he's around?"

Jan sat up.

"Listen, Tina. Go and get your gear on. It's only half nine. There's another three hours at least. You go. Go on." She pulled Tina's slack body from the settee.

Tina looked at Jan, eyes wide, childish.

"Do you mean it? I was – I mean – to you."

"Oh, give over, Tina. It was partly my fault it all

happened, trying to be clever. Look, be a pal and get ready and go on."

"Suppose he comes back?"

"Well, you've got a poker in the fireplace, haven't you? If he tries to be funny with me, or the kids, I'll belt him one."

Tina looked at her. "You would, too, wouldn't you?"

She left the room and twenty minutes later was ready to go.

"I don't think they'll wake up, honest, Jan. But if they do, their things are in the cupboard there and . . ."

"Oh, go on, Tina, or you'll turn into a pumpkin."

When Tina had gone, Jan switched on the box and switched it off again. They save all the rubbish until everyone's too drunk to care, she thought.

She was dozing when she heard a little whimpering sound from the passage. The door opened more widely. A little girl, pyjamas at half-mast, thumb in mouth, peeped round the corner, eyes round.

Jan spread her arms.

"Come on, Button."

The small body, smelling warmly of pee and perspiration curled up in her lap.

They were both asleep, holding on to one another when Tina came back.

37

On New Year's Day, Mrs Elsom and Jan went out along the river. The pale, washed sky curved down to vanish into soft haze on the western horizon, where the sun set, gently orange. Now trees were bare the landscape showed through and distant woods were dark and brooding.

Sparrows chattered lazily in the bushes. Everywhere was still and no one else was about. They walked quietly, arm in arm.

"Are you really comfortable in that attic, our Jan?" asked the old woman at last.

"Snug as a bug in a rug."

They passed the allotments.

"Hey, look at that."

Jan pointed to the yellow-green shoots pointing through the dark soil.

"That's the broad beans, love. There's a lot grows in winter. Look t'ee."

She indicated a cottage hedge where small yellow blossoms stood out amid the green.

"Winter jasmine. Eh, and look."

She pulled Jan to the gate and pointed to the dark earth under the window sill, now spotted with green.

"Daffs coming through."

"Get away."

"True. Hope the frost doesn't get them."

They reached the street, walking slowly. By now Jan had learnt to adjust her stride to Edie's short bird-like steps. She felt her arm squeezed.

"Jan love, are you really going to look for your mother?"

"That's my New Year Resolution"

"Eh, love. I hope it'll turn out all right."

"I don't know. But I'm doing it."

They closed the street door behind them. The house still smelt of paint and paste.

"It's a mess."

"No it's not."

"Oh it is. But it'll be all right come February. Look, Jan, you go on up and see to yourself. I'm going to make a nice supper, then we'll see the New Year in later on."

"I'll give you a hand."

"No you'll not."

Jan climbed to her attic room. The door opened and shut and she was closed into her little white world. The setting sun threw one diagonal beam across the wall. She went over to the east-facing window and sat down on a cushion, arms round her knees.

In the far distance she could see something paler above the dark moors. There was snow on Borley Top. They were truly into winter now. She stared out while the light faded and the room darkened behind her. Then she reached back onto the bed, pulled her bag down and slid out the postcard. The face of the older woman looked at her, shy and shamed.

Who is now the mother, who the daughter?

But it was Dad who came into her mind. In just a week since she had moved out, her anger and resentment had faded. He was not meant for anger, not from his daughter. Women had always cared for him, hadn't they? First Gran then Mum, then when Mum went, Jan took over. And now here was Sandra stepping forward to do her bit. There was no end to it, she thought, and no end to his need and wish to be looked after.

But Mum, she had run away like a bad girl, and gone wandering through the world. She'd run away from Dad, and Kev, and David Thompson too if Margaret Hardwick guessed right. She couldn't gather men around her. And no one was coming round to meet her every need, were they?

Oh, if Jan ever had a daughter, she would tell her. You may not have a man in your life, but everyone has a woman in theirs.

The dark moors melted into darker evening and still she did not move to light the inner darkness of the room.

She was on her own now. But not alone in her thoughts. Somewhere out there, somewhere over Borley Top, was Mum. She knew that. She had known all along that Mum was there, just beyond the edge of her life. Perhaps she sat by a window and thought long thoughts about herself and what had gone before and what was to come.

She was there, somewhere, and Jan would find her and things would be – well, they'd see.